*Other Avon Camelot
Science Fiction Titles:*

JEROME BEATTY, JR. has written several books
for young people. A former newspaperman and magazine editor, his articles have appeared in many publi-
cations, including *The Saturday Review,* where he
wrote the Trade Winds column. Born in New York,
Mr. Beatty was graduated from Dartmouth College.
He now lives on Cape Cod with his family.

Matthew Looney And The Space Pirates

by JEROME BEATTY, JR.

Pictures by GAHAN WILSON

AN AVON CAMELOT BOOK

AVON BOOKS
A division of
The Hearst Corporation
959 Eighth Avenue
New York, New York 10019

Text Copyright © 1972 by Jerome Beatty, Jr.
Illustrations Copyright © 1972 by Gahan Wilson.
Published by arrangement with Young Scott Books,
a division of Addison-Wesley Publishing Company, Inc.
Library of Congress Catalog Card Number: 72-179371.
ISBN: 0-380-00848-3

First Camelot Printing, February, 1974.
Fourth Printing

CAMELOT TRADEMARK REG. U.S. PAT. OFF.
AND IN OTHER COUNTRIES,
MARCA REGISTRADA, HECHO EN U.S.A.

Printed in the U.S.A.

Table of Contents

1. The Collector

The two Moonsters stood on the edge of the tiny crater and looked down.

"What a mess!" exclaimed the one called Izdor.

Across the floor of the crater were spread pieces of metal of all sizes and shapes. There didn't seem to be any sense to the way they were laid out.

"Those Earthlings are the sloppiest creatures in the Universe," declared Lubbock, the second Moonster.

The two of them walked down the slope to inspect the scene more closely.

"Every time they visit us, this is the way they leave things," Izdor said. "Not only here but up there, too." He pointed over his head. "There are scads of dangerous contraptions flying around. It isn't safe any more."

"Hey, look at this!" Lubbock had found a gadget resting on three legs, with a round screen and a long wand sticking out of it. A shiny box was giving off clicking and humming noises.

"It's sending back signals," Izdor said.

"Let's smash it."

"Don't you dare! My job is to report on what we found, and that's all. Besides, if you did that, it would probably bring them back sooner."

Lubbock was disappointed, but agreed. "Okay. But they'll come back when they want to, anyway. They always do."

Izdor spent a lot of time shooting spectrophonic pictures and writing notes. Lubbock, who was a pilot and not a scientist, wandered about. Once he picked up an object, looked it over, and muttered something about "those doggone earth people."

"Put that down," Izdor ordered him. "We're not to disturb anything."

"What's the difference?" Lubbock grumbled, dropping the object. "They've left stuff all over the Moon, and you scientific guys still haven't figured out how to stop them."

"You're impatient, aren't you?"

"The Earthlings are going to take our Moon away from us, and you tell me I'm impatient." Lubbock made a disgusted face.

Izdor put his spectrophone and notebook away. "Come on, let's go. I'm finished."

They went up out of the crater and walked about half a lunacule to where they had parked the mola-copter. On the way, Lubbock argued some more.

"Look," he said, "you brainy types think you can make a deal with the Earthlings, don't you? That you can tell them when and where to land, and how long to stay, and so on?"

"Sure. We'll make them understand that the Moon is ours, just as the Earth is theirs. If they want to come here, they must obey our laws."

"But each time they come here they do exactly as they please. They haven't paid any attention to our signals."

Izdor looked at him. "How would you handle it?"

"I'd blast 'em! I'm sick and tired of this pussy-footing. The only language they understand is force. Drop one or two of our Lava bombs in the right places, and they'll think twice about messing up our moon-scape again." He stared up at the Earth. "And besides, it's so ugly."

His companion laughed. "What's that got to do with it? I'm sure Earthlings think the Moon is ugly. It all depends on where you live, I guess. As for firing a Lava bomb, it would kill innocent people. We Moonsters wouldn't do that, no matter what. You'll

9

have to trust our leaders. Right now they are thinking of a way to save the Moon."

"They'd better think fast," Lubbock said. "There isn't much time left."

By this time they had reached the molacopter. They climbed in. Lubbock, in the pilot's seat, pressed buttons and turned knobs. Finally, the little machine rose and flew quietly away. Lubbock set a course over the Rook Mountains and across the Ocean of Storms. In about forty-five moonits they would reach Crater Copernicus, the capital of the Moon, where Izdor would report to the Commission on Cosmic Affairs.

After the two visitors had gone, the area fell silent again. This was a deserted part of the Moon, far from the nearest town. It would have surprised Izdor and Lubbock to know that they had been watched. As their molacopter flew out of sight, a third Moonster stepped out from behind a huge rock, walked over to the crater and looked down at the Earth litter spread out below. He rubbed his hands together and smiled. Then he hurried away, climbing down into one of the other little craters nearby. Soon there was a chugging sound, and he reappeared at the wheel of a lunabile. He drove it over the rim and down to where all the Earth litter was. He parked it next to the three-legged transmitter. On the side of the lunabile was a very large sign:

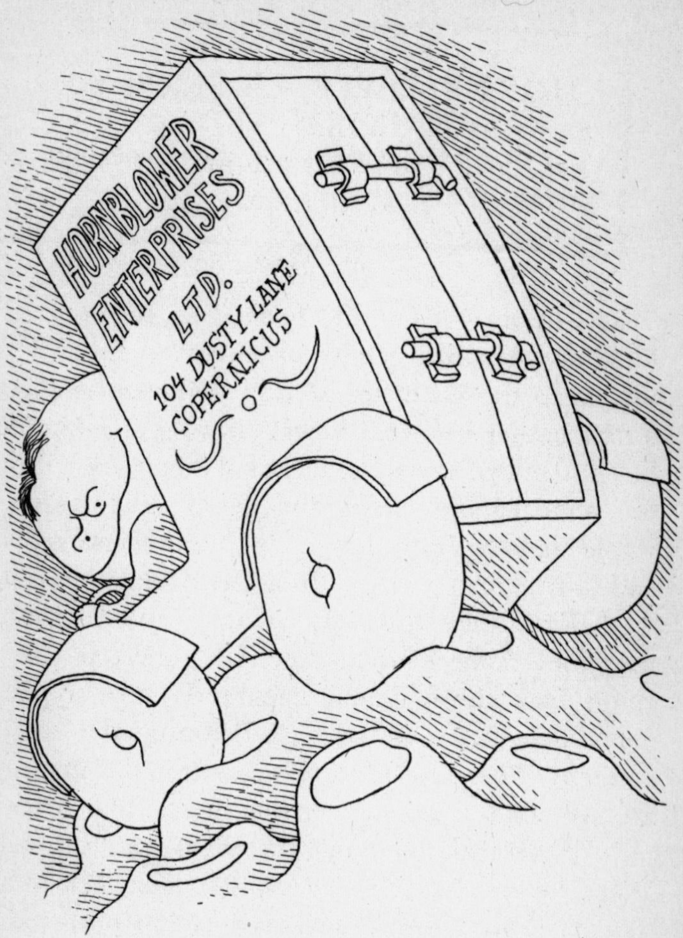
HORNBLOWER
ENTERPRISES
LTD.
104 DUSTY LANE
COPERNICUS

He reappeared at the wheel of a lunabile.

The driver got out and opened up the back of the lunabile, revealing plenty of storage room. Then he turned to the Earth transmitter and took it apart. It didn't bother him that it was clicking and humming. He just pulled the wires out of the box, took the legs off, removed the screen and aerial, and packed the whole shebang into his vehicle. He then walked back and forth, picking up anything that looked interesting. The Earthlings had left all sorts of complicated machines. Some of them were little gadgets that you could look through and apparently take a picture. Some were fancy bottles with delicate tubes attached to them. There were quite a few things stuck in the ground with wires connecting them. The Moonster pulled them all out and put them in his lunabile. When he got through, there wasn't much left to show that Earthlings had landed. He had to push hard to force the lunabile doors closed on the collection. He climbed into the driver's seat and started the engine.

The lunabile chugged up the side of the crater. It was heavily loaded, and it went very slowly. The driver looked worried, but finally, with a lurch, it went over the top and onto the level moon surface. The driver broke into a big smile, shifted into higher speed, and shouted happily, "Hector Hornblower rides again!"

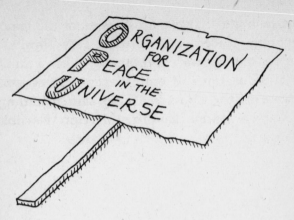

2. Matt's Plan

The inhabitants of the Moon were worried. For as long as they could remember they had lived in peace and quiet. There had never been trouble with any other people in the galaxy. And now, suddenly, Earthlings were invading. They landed without warning, each time bringing more and more equipment with them. It certainly looked as though they planned to take over the planetoid for themselves.

Moonsters argued over how to deal with the menace. Some believed that war should be declared and that all foreign spaceships should be shot down as they came near. The Anti-Earth League wanted to go even further. Its members wanted to fire Lava bombs at Earth until it shriveled up. That would end the nuisance for good. There was no doubt that the powerful weapons of the Space Navy could easily wreck the spaceships and launching pads used by the Earthlings. Then there was another group called the Organization for Peace in the Universe. They said that the only way to keep anyone from getting hurt was for the Moon's population to move far away. (The Anti-Earthers always made fun of this organization by holding their noses and calling it by its initials— O.P.U.)

But many Moonsters were not sure what should be done. They didn't much like the idea of war. And they weren't too happy at the thought of moving to some strange corner of the galaxy. So they went about their business and hoped that the leaders of the government would figure out what was best.

The capital of the Moon, Crater Copernicus, was full of confusion and excitement. Important officials rushed back and forth from one cave building to another. They carried secret papers and orders. In the streets there often were crowds protesting. The Anti-Earthers marched back and forth chanting their slogans, such as:

"Hey di Hey!
Ho di Ho!
That ugly Earth
Has got to go!"

Those belonging to the Organization for Peace in the Universe were quieter. They kept a picket line going in front of the Capitol Cave. The pickets carried signs such as this one:

WE'RE NOT DYING TO SAVE THE MOON. ARE YOU?

Whenever government officials came to their offices in the Capitol Cave, they had to push their way through the crowd. The mob made the most noise when it recognized members of the Commission on Cosmic Affairs. That was because they were supposed to be deciding what to do about the Earth invasions. Sometimes the Royal Moonties had to be called out to protect the commissioners when they came and went. The Commission was made up of scientists and politicians and military brass. Among them was Chairman of the Moon (that's similar to President) R. T. Muss. There was bearded old Professor Ploozer, the genius whose discoveries made it possible for Space Navy ships to roam the universe. And there was young Matthew Looney, now a full commander in the Navy, and the Moonster who perhaps knew most about the Earth. He had been there three times. He had also traveled to other distant places. His uncle, the famous explorer, Lockhard "Lucky" Looney, had taken Matt on many space treks. Now Admiral Looney was retired, and his nephew was the leading figure in the Space Navy.*

The Commission on Cosmic Affairs did have an excellent plan for dealing with the Earth. It did not mean going to war, nor did it mean fleeing the Moon. The plan was to get the Earth to sign a treaty, in which it would agree to the following:

1. Not to land on the Moon without permission.
2. To land at spaceports instead of any old place they felt like.
3. Not to steal any more valuable minerals from private property.
4. Not to litter the moonscape.
5. To put no more junk in orbit around the Moon.
6. When arriving on the Moon, to go through customs and have all baggage inspected.

The Commission's plan was a good one, except for one trouble: it wasn't working. The Earth had never replied to any of the interspatial spectrophonic messages sent to it. When they got word of this latest arrival of Earthlings, the commissioners said, "Ah, this is it. They are sending an ambassador to sign the treaty." But before they could get ready to greet them, the Earthlings had taken off again without a word. Now the Commission sat in the conference room, deep in the Capitol Cave, and listened to Izdor's report.

* Their adventures are told in *Matthew Looney's Voyage to the Earth, Matthew Looney's Invasion of the Earth,* and *Matthew Looney in the Outback.*

"As usual," he told them, "a large amount of rubbish was left. Some of it was just thrown there, while some of it seems to have been placed carefully. Now, look at these, for instance."

Izdor placed his camera atop the spectrophonic projector, plugged it in, and aimed it at a big screen at the end of the conference room. One by one, he showed pictures of the site of the latest landing by the invaders from Earth.

"They left more behind than they ever have before," Chairman Muss noted.

"That's because they bring more with them each trip," Matt explained. "Sooner or later they will build a base, and then we'll never get rid of them."

Professor Ploozer pointed to the screen. "But every one of those gegadgets has some gepurpose." He spoke with a strange accent because he was from Ganymede, near Jupiter.

Izdor flashed the next picture on the screen.

"What's that gadget, Professor?" someone asked.

"Oh, that, well, it could be sending gesignals."

"It makes noises," Izdor said.

"Then I'm geright. It's a transgemitter."

When the pictures had all been shown and Izdor was finished, the members of the Commission started arguing again about what to do. They took all sides.

". . . they'll build a base and then we'll never get rid of them."

"Drop the bomb!" "No violence!" "No surrender!"

Chairman R. T. Muss rapped the hard shale table with his graphite stylus. "Gentlemen! Order, please!"

Professor Ploozer, who had fallen asleep for a few moonits, awoke with a start. "A well-gedone lavaburger, and a geside dish of fried puckles."

"My dear Ploozer," R. T. Muss said patiently, "we are talking about our Earth problem."

"Oh, sorry. I must have gedozed off," the professor said. His stomach rumbled.

"As I was about to say," R. T. Muss went on, "the situation doesn't look any better. Now I have all sides yelling for my scalp. But as long as I am Chairman of the Moon, we shall not start a war. Nor shall we pack up and leave our beloved sphere."

"What are we going to do, keep on with this crazy treaty scheme?" angrily cried a commissioner by the name of Gorky. "When they don't even pay any attention to us?"

"That is right." R. T. Muss turned toward Matt. "Commander Looney, have you anything to say now that you've heard the report by Izdor?"

Matt was wearing the uniform of the Space Navy. He stood up and cleared his throat. "These are difficult times for our Moon. This new landing certainly shows they mean business. It has been discouraging, trying to parley with the Earth people. And I know them. They are tricky. Yet, we must keep on trying."

"That's exactly what you told us at the last meeting," Gorky snarled. "Haven't you had a new idea since then?"

"Well, yes, I have."

"What is it, Commander?" R. T. Muss asked.

"So far Earth has not answered any of our messages sent by interspatial spectrophone. Maybe they aren't being received. Now, I see that one of the devices left behind this time is a transmitter. I could try to contact Earth with it. I have a very good friend—Dr. Leonard O. Davinchy—who is connected with their space program. Some of you met him when he visited the Moon not long ago. If I could reach him through this transmitter, he would put me in touch with the right people to talk about the treaty."

"An excellent idea," cried R. T. Muss. "Don't you agree, Gorky?"

"Yeah, it might work," Gorky admitted grudgingly. "Better than sitting around here and arguing."

Matt sat down, and Ploozer patted his shoulder. "You always hit the genail on the head, my boy."

One night later—Moonsters like to keep out of the uncomfortable sunlight as much as possible—a large molacopter took off from the main spaceport. In it were Matt and several members of the Commission on Cosmic Affairs. Matt took extra phonic equipment to help work the transmitter left by the Earthlings.

Chairman Muss, seated next to him, said, "Matt, this is our last chance. It's got to work, or the Moon is in a real bad way."

Matt smiled. "Don't worry, it'll work. I've used Earth machines before."

Just about then, a lunabile with the sign "Hornblower Enterprises Unlimited" on it was chugging into Crater Copernicus on a back road. It had been a long, rough journey over the moonwastes. But the driver, Hector Hornblower, knew it would be worth it.

3. The Troublemaker

The commissioners were tired and disgusted when the big molacopter brought them back to Copernicus. They had flown halfway around the Moon and found only footprints, wheeltracks, and a few useless odds and ends at the Earthling landing site. To make things worse, there was a crowd waiting for them at the molaport. Somehow word had gotten around that the Commission was coming back with good news. When the Moonsters saw the unhappy faces of the commissioners, they knew it wasn't good, and they became unruly. The Royal Moonties held them back. Matt and the others climbed out of the flying machine and hurried away. Chairman Muss had warned them all not to talk to reporters. The situation was very tense, and more bad news would certainly make it even worse.

Matt went home for a rest. He lived with his parents, Mr. and Mrs. Monroe K. Looney, and his sister, Maria, in a comfortable cave house at 55 Canal Street. After Mr. Looney had retired as manager of the powder factory, the family had moved from their home in Crater Plato to be near Matt.

Matt pushed open the big stone door and walked inside. His father was there to greet him. "Well, how did it go?"

"Bad, real bad." The boy shook his head slowly, and told his father what had happened.

"Can't they find out who took the stuff?" Mr. Looney wanted to know.

"The gumshoes are working on it. But even if they do, we've missed a chance to contact Earth. It may be our last. If R. T. Muss doesn't come up with something, I think we're going to have a revolution. Where's Mom?"

"Out shopping."

"I'm tired, Dad. I'm going to bed."

Matt couldn't sleep right away. He tossed and turned and thought about the Moon's problems. If there was only more time, he was sure he could get his friends on Earth to talk over the treaty, and perhaps even sign it. If he could only reach them somehow. If he only had that transmitter. If—if—he finally fell sound asleep.

He was at the wheel of the giant spaceship Feebey. *"Prepare for landing," he ordered Mr. Bones, the mate. The blue-green Earth loomed ever closer. Matt twisted the wheel and the big craft floated toward the ground, but a voice bothered him. "Matthew! What's the matter?" A hand held his arm so he couldn't steer.*

He opened his eyes. He was still in bed, and his mother was leaning over him.

"Are you all right, son? You were carrying on so."

"Hi, Mom. Yeah, I'm all right. Just a dream." Matt yawned and stretched.

His mother straightened up and smiled. "You've been asleep all day and all night. Now get yourself dressed. I have some nice breakfast for you." She left.

Matt knew the reason for his dream. Lately he had been trying to get the Commission on Cosmic Affairs to send him to the Earth with the treaty. But they always said no. At the next meeting, he was going to ask again. He sat at the kitchen table and gobbled up a plate of scrambled arks and then ate a dish of burgles with canal juice. He was hungry. Mrs. Looney puttered around, smiling, while Matt ate. She liked to see her boy eat a hearty meal. Matt appreciated it, too, especially the flowers in the middle of the table. They were the season's first algies, those pretty green blooms you see on the mountain slopes. And look at the handsome aluminum vase.

"Guess." Mrs. Looney smiled.

Aluminum vase! There was only one place where aluminum came from! Matt grabbed it. "Where'd you get *this?*"

Mrs. Looney smiled some more. "Oh, do you like it? It's a nice surprise, isn't it?"

"But where, Mom? Where from?"

Mrs. Looney's smile faded, and she frowned a little. "Why, from the Earth, son. It's very rare, you know."

Matt tried to be patient. "Yes, I know. But where did you get it?"

"Oh, at this wonderful little shop. It's just filled with interesting things from other planets—"

"Other planets?"

"Well," Mrs. Looney said, "they're all from Earth, come to think of it. And guess what? It's run by an old friend of yours."

"An old friend? Who?"

"Guess." Mrs. Looney smiled.

"No, Mom, I'm not going to guess. Tell me. This is important."

"Oh, all right. Hector Hornblower. You remember him."

Matt felt as though a meteorite had dropped on his head. *Hector Hornblower.* Remember him? How could he ever forget that bubble-headed loudmouth? Hector Hornblower had caused Matt more trouble than you can imagine. On the Moon, in space, and on Earth.

The last Matt had heard, Hector had flunked out of the Mooniversity again and was singing and playing the moondolin in a day club in Crater Plato. (He was talented, Matt admitted.) He and Matt had gone to school together, and they had joined the Space Navy at the same time. Matt kept getting promoted, while Hector went in the other direction. When he got to the lowest rank there was—Cabin Boy, Ninth Class— he quit. And now it looked as though he was mixed up in some more shenanigans. Oh, boy, Matt thought, as if we don't have enough to worry about!

"—and he was so helpful." Matt's mother was still talking about Hector. "He showed me how to un- screw the end off this bottle and make a vase out of it, and—"

"Mom, please. Tell me where the store is."

"Well, let me see. You go out Newton, turn left on Kepler. There's this little road called Dusty Lane. Hector's place is—"

"I'll find it," Matt called, as he rushed out the door.

The fastest way to go a short distance on the Moon is to peddle. You bend your knees in a certain way, and you push with your toes. You lean forward, and you move your arms back and forth as though you were hauling on a long rope. On the Moon, where the gravity is weak, peddling will take you along rather nicely. If you don't do it right, though, you can find yourself going in the wrong direction—up. Then you waste a lot of time getting your feet back on the moonscape again. In the evenings you often see kids floating around over your head, calling for someone to help them. They were in such a hurry to get home from school that they tried to peddle, without knowing how, and got stuck.

Matt peddled as fast as he could in the direction of Dusty Lane. When he got there, he could see why they called it that. It was a short, dusty little road that didn't seem to go anywhere, ending in front of a big lava mound that rose above the moonscape. And that's where the action was, as Matt could plainly see. Moonsters were gathered in front of a little cave store. A big sign proclaimed as follows:

HORNBLOWER ENTERPRISES UNLIMITED
Souvenirs from Earth!
Genuine Leftovers From the Latest Landing
AUTHENTIC

Cash   No Refunds

Laid out in front of the shop were all sorts of Earth-made goods. People were looking them over and, if they saw something they liked, they took it inside. Matt went in and heard a cash register ring. The cave was lit by sulphur torches stuck in the walls. On the shelves was more stuff for sale. Matt heard Hector's familiar voice.

"Hurry! Hurry! Hurry! Get 'em while they last!" He gave a customer a package he had just wrapped. "That'll be forty rubbles, lady. Thank *you!*" He rang it up. Matt was now standing beside him. "What'll it be, mister?"

Matt was angry, but controlled himself. "Just what do you think you're doing?"

Hector recognized his friend. "Why, if it ain't my old pal Looney!" A big grin split his round face. "How's the space racket these days?"

Matt got to the point. "What right did you have to steal these things and put them on sale?"

Hector stopped grinning. "Now, just wait a moonit, fella. Steal is a mighty big word. This stuff don't belong to nobody except the one that's smart enough to get his hands on it, and that happens to be me, Heck Hornblower. And if you wanna get legal about it, the real owners are back on Earth. So what do you say about that?"

"What I say, wise guy, is that you ruined about the only chance we had of getting in touch with Earth. As usual, you've caused the Moon serious trouble."

"*As usual, you've caused the Moon serious trouble.*"

"Aw, cut it out, pal," Hector said with a smirk. "What trouble could this cause?"

"There was a transmitter. I was about to signal Earth with it."

"Why, you can have your transmitter," Hector said in a friendly tone. "Just pick it out. I'll let you have it ten per cent off, since you're my pal."

"Hornblower, you're such a—such a—" Matt couldn't think of the right insult. But if the transmitter was here, he might as well get his hands on it. He described it to Hector.

"Oh, *that*," Hector replied. "The round screen. A lady from Plato bought that. Gonna make a lamp out of it. No, I don't know her name or address. As for the aerial, some kid took it. Going fission, he said."

"What about the box with the machinery in it?" Matt asked hopefully.

Hector shrugged his shoulders. "I took it apart. Wanted to see what made it tick. Not much left of it now."

Matt finally blew up. He shook his fist at Hector. "This is too much!"

Hector said, "Go ahead, threaten me. You and your fancy uniform. There's no reason why the rest of us shouldn't make a little something for ourselves on this space racket."

"You just keep yourself out of our business from

now on, Hornblower!" Matt stomped out of the cave, which he shouldn't have done, because he bumped his head on the ceiling.

Hector rubbed his hands together and smiled. "So they've got more business? That's where Hornblower Enterprises Unlimited moves in."

4. An Intruder

Nothing could be done about the stolen transmitter.
Matt reported it to the police, but they said Hector
hadn't broken any law. The unrest on the Moon was
getting so bad that politicians were afraid to go out into the streets. Even Matt was worried that some of the
Anti-Earthers might beat him up. So when the next
meeting of the Commission on Cosmic Affairs was
held, he took a back way to the Capitol Cave. Pickets
and protesters blocked the main entrance. The Royal
Moonties let Matt in a side door. He was late. As it
turned out, he had missed the most interesting part.

"Ah, Commander," Chairman R. T. Muss said,
"just in time for the news."

"The news?"

"Yes. It's all settled. You're going on a space trip."

Matt's heart leaped with joy. He was always glad to get away from the dull life in the capital and out into the excitement of space. But what made him happier was that the Commission had finally agreed to his idea: to send him to the Earth to make peace.

R. T. Muss put an arm around Matt's shoulder. "Come here, young man, and I'll show you something." He led the way to a huge map of the galaxy on the wall. He picked up a pointer. "Now, here is our little Moon here. And there is the lopsided Earth."

"It won't take long to get there," Matt said eagerly.

"And here—" R. T. Muss moved the pointer away over to the other corner of the big chart. "—is the Hercules Globular Cluster, your destination." He smiled at the bewildered young spaceman.

"The Hercules Glob—what do you mean? Why there?"

"Sit down, Commander, and I'll explain." Matt took a chair. "The Commission has just decided that for the good of the Moon we must give in to the agitators, for the time being."

"Give in? But that's—"

R. T. Muss held up a hand, and went on. He told Matt that an expedition would be sent to the Hercules Globular Cluster. It would be partly a colonizing expedition, to please the Organization for Peace in the

35

Universe. And it would also set up a military base, which would make the Anti-Earthers happy.

"A great spot to fire Lava bombs at the Earth from," Gorky said. "Too far for them to shoot back."

"And while you're on your mission," R. T. Muss said, "things will quiet down here and give us more time to talk things over with Earth."

Matt went over to the chart again. "Hercules is a very big place. Just where did you have in mind?"

R. T. Muss put his finger on a certain spot, "Right here, the same planet you and your uncle, Admiral Lockhard Looney, explored not long ago. It is called Freeholy, and reports are that it has a nice climate, no wild animals, and plenty of food."

"Freeholy, eh?" Matt took a red ribbon and tacked one end on the Moon's location. Then he stretched it across to where Freeholy was and tacked it again. "Hmmm. Quite a distance. Crosses some wild territory. Long trip. Well, sir, we'll do our best." He snapped a salute at R. T. Muss.

The chairman grabbed Matt's hand and shook it. "I know you will, my boy."

The other commissioners crowded around Matt and wished him well. Then R. T. Muss spoke again in a very serious tone.

"I must caution you all. This is to remain top secret until the expedition leaves. No one except the leaders must know that Freeholy is the planet we have picked. We don't want a whole new round of protests to come up over our choice."

A project this big could not be kept secret for long. Soon it was all over the Moon that Matt would lead the trek into space. The magazine *Northern Lights* interviewed him. The *Copernicus Gazette* had an editorial which stated that Chairman Muss had done the right thing. The crowds in the street were more friendly. Whenever Matt entered the Capitol Cave, or showed up at the spaceport at the Sea of Crisis, Moonsters cheered him on. He was glad, because he had a lot of preparations to make, and he couldn't have done a good job with a bunch of pickets bothering him all the time.

In spite of the publicity, no one but Matt and a few others knew exactly where the expedition was headed. Most Moonsters didn't care. They were happy enough that something was being done. But there was at least one who did care.

One night, just before the sun started to come up, Matt finished working on charts in the conference room. He locked up, walked through the long halls of the Capitol Cave, and out the front door. A small group of admirers clapped politely. Matt was too tired to notice one who couldn't clap because he held a pail of cleaning powder in one hand and a mop in the other. He had a short black beard and a mustache, a hat pulled over his ears, and wore a baggy, rumpled suit. A brush stuck out of one pocket and rags out of another. The crowd broke up, everybody going down the street except this fellow. He shuffled to the entrance of the Capitol Cave. There a Royal Moontie stopped him.

"Do you have an appointment, sir?"

"Cleaning man," mumbled the other.

"Oh, yes. Go right in."

Once inside, the cleaning man stopped shuffling and walked rapidly. He seemed to know where he was going, and soon came to the locked door of the conference room. He knocked. No answer. He put down his pail and mop, took out a skeleton key, and let himself into the room. He locked the door behind him, and then looked excitedly around. He rushed to the charts that Matt had left lying on the big table and went through them. He seemed puzzled, as though he couldn't understand them. Then he glanced at the wall behind him. There on the big map of the galaxy was a bright red ribbon. The cleaning man put one finger on the Moon and slowly traced the ribbon across the heavens. It came to an end on—

"Freeholy!" the intruder exclaimed. "In the Hercules Globular Cluster!" He grabbed a stylus and wrote down on paper the exact location. Fourteen by

"Cleaning man," mumbled the other.

one hundred ten on the parallax, et cetera. He stuck the paper in his pocket. He let himself out of the conference room, picked up his mop and pail, and strolled away without anyone paying him any attention. As he did so, a grin appeared on his bearded face, and he muttered between his teeth, "Hector Hornblower rides again!"

Yes, it was indeed he, disguised. He had found out the expedition's secret. But what use would this clever fellow make of it? He shuffled along the cool corridors of Capitol Cave until he was far from the conference room. Finally he found what he was looking for. He stopped in front of a door that read: *Registrar of Deeds and Claims*. Hector walked in. There was only one person in the office, an old Moonster who sat at a desk piled high with papers. Hector looked at him, took a deep breath, and said, "I want to stake a claim to a planet."

5. *An Unexpected Passenger*

The Sea of Crisis Navy base was always a busy place. But now it was busier than ever. Right in the middle of the landing field the giant spaceship *Feebey* rested on its launching pad. For many days and nights Moonsters had been coming and going, putting supplies on board and working on the machinery. Now the countdown had begun. Very shortly the moonscape would shake as the mighty engines roared, sending the *Feebey* away into distant space.

Almost all passengers were on board. There were several families who would start a Moon colony on the new planet. There were some military men, along with their guns and ammunition, who would set up a military base. Then there was the crew, headed by Commander Looney, with Mr. Bones second in command, and Harry Stottle, chief engineer, in the engine room. Vice-Chairman-of-the-Moon Heckity, who had already been named governor of the new colony, was the highest-ranking civilian aboard.

A platform had been built next to the main hatch of the ship. It was draped with bright flags. Chairman R. T. Muss was making a farewell speech to a large group of Moonsters who had come to see the takeoff. Reporters and cameramen were there. Matt, Governor Heckity, and other officials stood on the platform, too.

"And so I say, friends," R. T. Muss declared, "this fine expedition will be one of the most important in the history of the Moon. These brave pioneers will travel to the far corner of the galaxy. And now, it is time for me to reveal where they are going."

The audience murmured in excitement. Mr. and Mrs. Looney perked up their ears, for they had never been told. Another Moonster was even more interested. It was Hector Hornblower. On the ground beside him was a suitcase.

"Our colony and military base," R. T. Muss announced, "will be in the Hercules Globular Cluster —on the planet Freeholy."

"Yippee!" Everyone turned toward Hector, who had let out the cry. He picked up his suitcase and pushed his way through the mob toward the front. He waved a sheet of paper over his head. "I was right! Lemme through! I'm going on this trip!"

R. T. Muss and the others stared in bewilderment as Hector climbed the steps to where they stood. When Matt saw who it was, he acted. "Hornblower," he ordered, "get out of here or I'll have you arrested."

"Can't you get this through your thick skull, Looney? I'm going along. Got my bag packed and everything."

"Don't say I didn't warn you." Matt signaled two Royal Moonties. They moved over and grabbed Hector's arms.

"Just a moonit," he said, trying to shake loose. "If I don't go, then you don't go, neither."

R. T. Muss spoke. "Just what is the meaning of this, young man?"

"Tell your goons to lay off, and I'll show ya." R. T. Muss had the Moonties release Hector, whereupon he shoved the paper under the Chairman's nose. "Read it and weep, Chairman. The reason I'm going to Freeholy is a real good one—*I own it.*"

R. T. Muss looked at the document while the others read over his shoulder.

"Ridiculous!"

"Outrageous!"

"Not a very funny joke," Matt said.

"It ain't supposed to be funny," Hector replied.

"Is it legal?" someone asked R. T. Muss.

> ## CERTIFICATE OF TITLE
> To all Moonsters, Greeting: Know Ye that for the sum of one rubble, the Registrar of Deeds and Claims does give, grant, and sell to:
>
> *Hector H. Hornblower*
>
> All that parcel of planet known as: *Freeholy, in the Globular Cluster of Hercules,* to Have and to Hold Forever.
>
> In Witness thereof, I have hereunto set my hand and seal.
>
> Registrar
>
> *Wesley Wubbenhorst*

The chairman held the certificate up to the light, turned and twisted it this way and that, felt the seal with his fingers, and said, "Looks legal to me."

"Of course, it's legal!" Hector barked.

"You see," R. T. Muss explained to the others, "anyone can buy an uninhabited, unclaimed heavenly body. Hardly anyone does it, because there's usually no way to get to the property."

Hector Hornblower took the certificate from R. T. Muss, picked up his suitcase and walked aboard the *Feebey*. "I got a way to get to my property," he declared. "Now let's shove off!"

The officials had no choice. And so, after the farewells were said, the engines of the mighty spaceship *Feebey* roared. With Commander Matthew Looney at the helm, she blasted off for the long, hazardous journey through the wilds of the galaxy. Matt was so busy on the bridge that he hardly had a chance to think about having Hector aboard. He didn't want to think about it, because it made him so angry that he couldn't concentrate on flying.

But the time finally came when the blast-off was finished, and the spaceship flew itself. Mr. Bones was at the wheel, but he didn't have to do much. The astroputer did the work of choosing direction and speed, making sure the *Feebey* was on course. It was quiet on board, except when the meteor-repeller clicked every so often. Even the engines could not be heard, for the ship sped along on its own momentum. The only time any power was needed was when the astroputer called for a slight change in the course, or when the man at the wheel had to steer around some obstacle. In the engine room, Chief Engineer Harry Stottle and his men were ready for such emergencies.

At last Matt was able to relax. But only for a moonit, as he realized that he was going to have to deal with Hector Hornblower. He had put Wondervon Brown, chief cook and steward, in charge of finding Hector a place to stay. He called Brown to the bridge.

*The astroputer did the job of choosing
direction and speed.*

"Yah, I put der little pipsquirt into stateroom X-14," Brown told Matt. "Moved der people into anudder place." Brown always carried a big soupspoon with him, and he shook it. "Any more fresh lip from dot Hornbloomer, und I pot him on der noggin."

"I know how you feel, Brown, but we're going to have enough trouble as it is. Leave it to me. I'll go below and talk some sense into him."

That was quite a promise, Matt knew, but nevertheless he meant to try. He found his way to Hector's cabin, where he got another surprise. Pasted to the door was a sign:

Hector Hornblower, Real Estate
Lots for Sale on the
Beautiful Planet Freeholy
Knock and Enter

Matt knocked and entered. Hector was seated at a table, drawing lines and writing on a huge sheet of paper.

"Why, if it ain't our commander. Just in time for the good news."

"Good news to you, Hector, is usually bad news for the rest of us," Matt sighed.

"What do ya mean? Look here. Just got through naming a street after ya."

Matt now saw that Hector was drawing up a map of Freeholy, naming streets and numbering the lots. Sure enough, there was one called Looney Lane. It was a very short street. Matt looked more closely and saw it led to the town dump.

"Thanks a lot," he muttered.

"Aw, that ain't nothing. Glad to help out a friend. Now after I get these maps finished, I got another big project. You got a printing press aboard this heap, ain't ya?"

"Yes, why?"

"Great! Well, we're gonna need mooney, ain't we?" I'm printing up some three-rubble and nine-rubble bills. Gonna have a pitcher of Freeholy on one side, probably, and my pitcher on the other. What do you think of that?"

"I don't know. You'll have to ask Governor Heckity."

Hector reached into his suitcase and brought out a bottle. "I ain't worried. Everything's gonna be just munky-mory, Looney. Here, how about a snort of firmamented canal juice, just for old time's sake?"

"No, thanks. I'm on duty. If I were you I'd be careful of that stuff. It's powerful."

Hector took a swig. "What I do is *my* business, pal."

48

"What I came to tell you, Hector, is that I'm in command of this spaceship, and everyone on board this ship must obey my orders. That includes you."

Hector stood up and poked a finger in Matt's chest. "And what I want to tell you, fella, is that I'm just as much in command of this here expedition as you. You couldn't even go to Freeholy if I didn't say okay."

"All right, wise guy, why don't you go up to the bridge and take charge?"

"Because I'm too busy, that's why. But if things don't go right, maybe I will!"

When Matt stalked out, he slammed the door. Hector the troublemaker was going to be a real problem.

6. The Red Danger

But things didn't turn out as badly as Matt thought they would. At least, not right away. Hector didn't bother the men on the bridge, and the *Feebey* sailed along toward Freeholy without anything much happening. This part of the universe was fairly deserted. They never saw any traffic at all, although a few times the lunar scanner showed some foreign vessel far, far away. Probably a freighter carrying goods from one galaxy to another. Each day Matt wrote something in the log, like: "Covered 40,000 megacules. Course same as yesterday."

At regular times he would contact the Moon by interspatial spectrophone, so those back home would know how the voyage was going.

It was so peaceful that Matt began to worry. He didn't want anyone to know it, but he was superstitious.

One morning (Moon Time, of course) he sat in his chair on the bridge shuffling a deck of galactic cards.

Mr. Bones, at the helm, asked, "What be you up to now, Commander?"

"It's all too easy, Mr. Bones. There must be a catch. I'm going to read my fortune and find out what it is."

The first mate shrugged his shoulders and smiled. Matt put thirteen cards in a circle and piled the rest in front of him, face down. He turned them, mixed them around, and muttered:

"Castor, Pollux, Dingo, Mars,
Is there a message in the stars?
Corvus the Crow, Sign of the Bubble,
Are we going to have terrible trouble?"

Matt stared at the layout in front of him. He slowly placed a seven of crabs onto an eight of fish. After making a few more moves, he pointed at the cards. "Look, Mr. Bones. Look at that."

Mr. Bones took the pipe out of his mouth. "No use, Skipper. I can't read the cards, even if I did believe in 'em. What does it say?"

"The way I read it: 'Beware of the red danger.' "

The old salt chuckled. "I wouldn't listen to them pasteboards, young feller." Mr. Bones was much older than Matt, and had known him since he was a child.

Sometimes he forgot to use the formal language of the Space Navy. "And even if there do be a red danger out in the wilds of this universe, we'll handle it, don't you fret."

Just at that point Sparks, the spectrophone operator, appeared on the bridge. He handed Matt a piece of paper.

"Message for you, sir, from Headquarters." Matt read it.

"There you are, Mr. Bones!" he exclaimed, jumping to his feet. "Just what the cards predicted." Bones read the message: PIRATES REPORTED IN YOUR AREA. ADVISE CAUTION.

Matt swung into action immediately. He told Sparks there would be no reply to the message. Nor would any more messages be sent until further notice.

"Other spaceships can easily locate us by tuning in on our wave length."

"Aye, aye, sir." Sparks saluted and went to lock up the spectroroom.

Sweeping up the galactic cards and shoving them into his pocket, Matt then spread charts out on the navigator's table. He pressed several buttons on the astroputer. The machine quickly sent out a sheet of paper with the *Feebey's* position printed on it. Matt spent a long time with the calipers and ruler, marking the charts. Finally he spoke.

Just at that point Sparks appeared.

"All right, Mr. Bones, that seems to be the safest route. Through the Horsehead Nebula. We'll have to change course, and it will use up a little more fuel, but it will hide us for several days, until we're out of danger."

The Horsehead Nebula is a tremendous black cloud that covers a large area in the galaxy. Most spaceships avoid it, if possible, because it means flying blind for a long period of time. But Matt had been through it once before, with his uncle, Admiral Looney. And with the fine instruments on the *Feebey,* he was sure he could make it this time. He fed the information into the astroputer, which soon gave out the new course.

"One-forty-four on the cosmograph, Mr. Bones," Matt ordered, "and twelve-point-five by parallax."

"Aye, aye, sir." The mate turned the wheel, and the *Feebey*'s engines swung her onto the other course.

There were other precautions to take. Matt ordered the military troops to keep their weapons loaded. The *Feebey* was not a battleship, by any means, but there was a big cosmic ray gun mounted in the bow. Matt saw to it that it was loaded. Not that he wanted to endanger lives by engaging in a gunfight, but it never hurt to be ready. Matt accomplished all these things without telling the passengers because he didn't want to alarm them. After all, the chances were very slim that they would see any pirates.

The only Moonster who was suspicious was Hector Hornblower. He wondered why the spectroroom was locked. It didn't worry him too much, though, because he had his skeleton key. He went in whenever he felt like it. Sparks was never there, so Hector himself sent messages to the real estate office he had set up back on the Moon.

As the *Feebey* sped toward the protection of the Horsehead, Matt regularly aimed the lunar scanner all around the heavens. The screen showed nothing but a few meteors and asteroids. Finally the time came when the black nebula loomed ahead.

"All right, Mr. Bones, remember, we shall fly by lunar scanner. Watch this screen and make sure we don't ram some uncharted star."

The ship shot into the Horsehead Nebula and was engulfed in blackness. The lunar scanner showed far enough ahead so that the helmsman could steer around obstacles. On and on the moonship raced through the darkness. The only way to tell time was by the calendar clock. Matt and Mr. Bones took turns on the bridge. They watched the charts carefully to see where they were at all times.

"Well, Mr. Bones," Matt said one day, "we're almost to the other side of the nebula, according to the astroputer."

"If they be any freebooters, we've given them the

slip, you can be sure of that," the mate replied cheerfully. Then suddenly he stiffened. "Here, here, what have we got now? He stared at the scanner image. It showed a very large object directly in their path.

Matt studied the screen. "Another one of those stray asteroids. Bear off a little to starboard."

The mate twisted the wheel. But the asteroid moved and still blocked the way. It could have been the pull of gravity causing that. Only five thousand lunacules away and the *Feebey* was closing the distance fast.

"Better slow down," Matt ordered. Mr. Bones signaled the engine room. "Now take her to port," Matt said. But the asteroid moved that way, too. "Reverse engines!" Mr. Bones signaled again. The *Feebey* lurched and slowed even more. Right at this time the blackness of the Horsehead Nebula began to give way to a lighter scene. On the scanner the asteroid changed appearance. It seemed to be long and narrow.

"Stop engines!" Matt ordered.

Then the moonship slid gently out of the nebula's inky grasp. Mr. Bones and Matt took their eyes from the scanner screen and peered directly through the spaceshield to see what was in front. It was a spaceship! A sleek spaceship, different from any Matt had ever seen. From one end flew the skull and crossbones, the universal flag of piracy. On her bow was her name: *Adventurer of the Universe*. Her portholes were open and the barrels of solar guns were aimed at the *Feebey*. Then a strange voice crackled over the speaker on the bridge.

"Heave to! Or we'll blast you into the next cosmos!"

There was nothing else Matt could do. As he signaled the engine room, he said, "I hope you've noticed the color of that ship, Mr. Bones."

"That I have," the mate replied.

It was red.

Once more, the cards were right.

7. Stranded

The moonship *Feebey,* up until now so peaceful and quiet, rang with the screams of frightened Moonsters and the triumphant cries of the space pirates. About twenty of them had swarmed aboard from the *Adventurer of the Universe* and had taken control. They filled sacks with all the booty they could get their hands on—precious metals, food, clothing, jewelry. One had found Hector's bottle of firmamented canal juice and was staggering about, singing a strange song.

On the bridge, the members of the crew and some of the passengers were lined up nervously, while the pirate captain ranted and raved, waving a cutlass.

"I'm Captain Morgus, and me and my men rule the cosmos! Right, me hearties?"

The pirates who were guarding the Moonsters shouted, "Right, Redbeard!"

The nickname was for obvious reasons. The fellow's hair grew long and red from his head and face. He was dressed like his followers, only a bit fancier. He wore a big three-cornered hat with a plume. Underneath it a red and white bandanna was wrapped around his unruly hair. His long coat had big, shiny buttons. A broad belt with a polished buckle held up his pantaloons and scabbard. He was tall and thin, but gave the appearance of strength, as well as meanness. Strangely, he and all the other pirates were barefooted.

"Ho! Ho! Ho!" he roared. "Thought ye could outfox old Redbeard, sneaking through the Horsehead, did ye? But we follered ye all the way, thanks to a slew of messages sent by some real-estate big shot named Hornblower."

Matt flinched. *Why, that so-and-so! Wait till I—*.

The pirate captain's voice interrupted his thoughts. "And where is this Hornblower?"

Hector raised his hand.

"Oh, ho!" Redbeard cried. "Now, tell me, are you in charge of this bunch of rabble?"

"Why, no, Mister—er—Captain Redbeard." Hector pointed to Matt. "He is." Hector then slunk behind the others where he couldn't be seen.

Matt stepped forward. "Matthew M. Looney, Commander in the Moon Space Navy. I demand that you release us, or you will be brought to justice for this act of piracy."

"Demand, do ye?" boomed the pirate leader. "We'll see about demanding. Now, what other goods have ye aboard that'll make Redbeard rich? Answer me!"

Matt glared right back. "There is nothing left aboard this ship that is of any value to you, Captain. I warn you, you will be punished for this."

"Redbeard!" came a cry from below. Everyone turned to look. A pirate stumbled up the ladder, out of breath, and gasped, "We opened the hold. It's full of supplies. Enough wealth there so we can all retire."

"We need those supplies for our existence," Matt declared. "Don't you touch them."

"Well, well, well," Redbeard said. "It looks like we have quite a prize here. We'll just take this whole fine ship right home with us. But first, we'll deal with young Looney here. Try to cross up Redbeard, will ye? Now we're going to teach you a lesson you'll never forget." His face was meaner than ever. He called to one of his men. "Gus, the plank!"

Gus, like the others, was wearing a jet tube. By means of it he shot out the hatch and over to the *Adventurer*, returning with a long board. They secured it to the open hatch so that it stuck out into space. Redbeard waved his cutlass at Matt.

"Demand, do ye?" boomed the pirate leader.

"All right, Looney! Take yourself for a little space walk! Out you go!"

Matt hesitated, but when the other pirates started sticking the points of their cutlasses into his back, he stepped onto the plank. Well, he thought, so be it. Perhaps by sacrificing himself, the rest of the expedition would get a break from the cruel Captain Redbeard.

The pirates were jeering and cackling with glee. Matt edged farther out on the plank, as Redbeard poked him with the cutlass. The shouts of the buccaneers inside the spaceship were now almost lost in the great silence of space. Matt looked up, down, and around. Stars and spiral galaxies surrounded him on all sides. It struck Matt as very pretty. Suddenly he began to lose his balance. Redbeard was stamping up and down on the other end of the board. It shook Matt loose. Slowly—there was little gravity—one foot went up, and his body began to tumble away, little by little. He heard Redbeard's "Ho! Ho! Ho!" as he gradually moved away from the spaceships. He had no control over the way he was moving. He turned his head and saw the plank being pulled in, and the hatch of the *Feebey* close. Then there was a puff of smoke and a red flash. The engines of the *Feebey* had been started. The moonship moved away, picking up speed. The *Adventurer of the Universe* gave off smoke and flames and followed the *Feebey*. Their exhaust blew Matt into a spin and sent him off in the other direction.

Soon both crafts were out of sight. There was silence.

Matt was alone. Suspended in the universe, half-way between the Moon and the Hercules Globular Cluster, he was helpless. He was probably moving slowly, but in what direction? And he would starve to death before he got anyplace. No two ways about it, Matt was doomed, and he knew it. Yet he couldn't quite believe it, and he decided not to give up hope. He went through his pockets and found a few items:

1 deck of galactic cards
1 copy of *Gloop's Guide to the Galaxy,* a travel book
2 bars of volcandy
1 stylus and notebook
1 AGM, an antigravity machine which controls the pull of gravity on a person
1 solar pistol

Interesting, but not of much use if you're lost in space. Matt stopped kidding himself, and got ready for the worst. He took out the notebook and stylus and wrote a report on what had happened. In case his body was ever found, it would be important to have a record. When he finished, he opened to a clean page and began a farewell note to his parents:

"Dear Mom and Pop: In case they find me, I want you to know—"

It was a sad letter, even though Matt tried to sound cheerful. He explained that his death was not a waste, because scientists could learn something from what happened to him. He reminded his mother and father that he had had a happy childhood and that he loved his family.

When the letter was written, Matt felt tired and hungry. He nibbled a bit of volcandy, and dozed off. He had no idea how long he had been sleeping, when he was awakened by a humming sound. The AGM had started working. That meant some large object was nearby! Maybe a planet where he could live until rescue parties found him! Matt looked around, but saw nothing. Then suddenly there it was. But it was only an asteroid, much too small to be of any help. Matt's hopes were dashed.

But as the thing grew nearer, he noticed something unusual. It was perfectly round and smooth. Matt put his AGM in reverse and he was pulled toward the asteroid. Then he realized *it was not an asteroid, but some sort of vehicle.* Matt touched it. He found what was a porthole and looked in. A faint glow lit up the interior. It was no bigger than his living room back home. He could barely see what was inside. There was the pilot's seat, but no one in it. A comfortable chair. A table with cups and dishes on it. Why was this empty vessel floating around out here? Where did it

A table with cups and dishes on it.

come from? Where in the universe do they make perfectly round spaceships?

The young Moonster's heart skipped a beat for joy. Maybe this abandoned craft was going to save his life! If he could get aboard, and if there was enough fuel, and if—

He worked his way back and forth on the outside of the ship, looking for an entrance. Finally, after much searching, he located a sort of handle. He pulled it and twisted it. A trap door flew open. Matt inched his way into the tiny opening, and the door shut automatically behind him. He tumbled onto the floor of the ship. He was inside.

He went to the cockpit. He had never seen anything like it. The instruments were marked in some strange language, and the controls were new to him. He searched for a chart, finding several of them laid out on a small navigator's table. They were written in the same strange language. Moonsters, as you may know from reading about their adventures in space, can speak and understand any cosmic tongue. But they cannot read them all. And this one was new to Matt.

But he was no dummy, After all, he had been first in his class at the Mooniversity. He wasn't a Space Navy Commander at his young age for no reason. He had already had a lot of experience. So, by a careful study of the charts—locating spacemarks and stars that he recognized—and by trying out the different gadgets he found on the navigator's table, Matt was able to fix his position. (It was of some help to know that he was in the general area of the Horsehead Nebula.)

Eagerly Matt prepared to send an S.O.S. to the Space Navy, to bring its ships quickly to rescue the *Feebey* from Captain Morgus. But he was in for a shock. He searched high and low and realized that there was no sending equipment aboard! The ship had been built for short trips. So there was only one thing to do: get back home as soon as possible. Matt bent over the charts again and marked a course for the Moon.

Now to start the engines. The control panel was a mystery to Matt. He took a chance and pushed a button. His seat fell back and almost threw him onto the deck. Another button brought the seat forward again. Other buttons worked the lights. Finally he pressed one and heard the humming sound of engines. Good! He twisted what looked like a speed knob, and felt the little ship start moving. He grabbed the wheel and turned it until he was on what he had figured was his course to the Moon. He got the craft going full speed, and hoped there was enough food and fuel on board to make the trip.

What did it matter? At least he was saved for the time being. He leaned back happily and cried, "Moon, here I come!"

Matt's joyous mood was a short one. He was in for still another shock. His sixth sense—which comes from living a life of excitement and danger—began to tell him something. He felt the back of his neck prickle. He was not alone on the spaceship! Slowly he reached for his solar pistol. From behind him there came a scream that made him almost jump out of his skin.

"Help! What are you doing in my space scooter! Get out!"

Matt quickly whipped out his gun and turned, ready to press the trigger, but stopped just in time. There was another passenger, all right, but it was an unarmed, female space person.

"A girl!" he exclaimed.

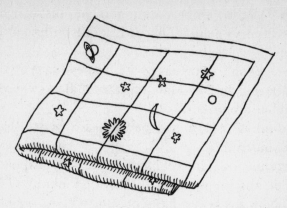

8. "You're Under Arrest!"

The main room of the space scooter was dimly lighted, but the surprised Moonster could see a tallish, thin creature in a green dress that fell almost to her knees. Her legs and feet were bare. Her skin was dark, compared to that of the pale-faced Moonsters. Her hair was long, shiny, and red. He could not see the color of her eyes, but they were big and round, and they stared at him.

"Of course it's a girl." She spoke more calmly now, in a pleasant voice. "What did you expect?"

"I didn't expect anybody. Where were you?"

"Asleep back there. Don't pretend you didn't know. And you can stop pointing that thing at me, whatever it is."

"Oh." Slightly embarrassed, Matt put his solar pistol away. "It's only a gun. There's just one bullet left in it, anyway."

"You've come to take me back, I guess," the girl said.

"Take you back?" Matt repeated. "Back where?"

"Back to Bolunkus."

"Bolunkus?" Matt had never heard of it. "Is that where you live?"

"Certainly it's where I live," the girl snapped. "I mean, it was where I *did* live, until I ran away from home. Now my father has sent you to bring me back."

"Well," Matt smiled, "I've got good news for you. You don't have to go back to Bolunkus. I'm not from there: I'm from the Moon. And that's where we're going."

"Don't try to fool me with that Moon stuff." The girl brushed past Matt and looked at the cosmic compass. "But this is the wrong direction. We're not going toward Bolunkus. My father didn't send you after me?"

"That's right," Matt said.

The girl suddenly collapsed into the armchair and started crying.

"But I thought you were running away," Matt said.

She looked at him through tears. "I am. But when a person runs away it's so that someone will catch her and bring her back. Daddy always does that. And now you've spoiled everything, you—you *kidnapper!*" She flopped down and cried some more.

The little scooter sped through the cosmos. Matt felt badly for the girl, but the most important thing now was to save the *Feebey* and its passengers. The only way to do that was to organize the Space Navy. He couldn't possibly put it off just because of some spoiled girl whose name he didn't even know.

"I'm sorry, miss," he told her. "I am on an important mission. When that is finished, I am sure we'll find a way to get you back home."

She paid no attention, just kept on blubbering. Matt checked the instruments. Everything was going fine. The girl's crying bothered him, so it was a while before he came to his senses and realized his mistake. Going all the way back to the Moon in this slow, little craft was silly. If there was a place nearby where he could contact the Moon he could save a lot of time. If that didn't work, he could rent a fast spaceship and make the trip in a hurry. He touched the girl on the shoulder.

"Come on, miss, pull yourself together. Where is this Bolunkus place, anyway? If it isn't too far, I'd like to go there."

The girl looked at Matt through tearful eyes and smiled. She jumped up, went to the navigator's table, and translated the chart for Matt. Bolunkus wasn't far, and with her help he soon had them heading that way.

She sat happily in the armchair. "You're from the Moon?" she asked. "Isn't that that dinky little place over on the other side of the galaxy? How did you happen to be floating in space all by yourself?"

Matt decided not to alarm the girl by telling her there were pirates in the area, so he said he had fallen overboard from a freighter. He found his homeland on one of the charts and told her about it, and also told her his name.

"Is it all right for me to call you Matthew?"

"Sure. And what shall I call you?"

"My name is Annalunkus."

"Okay, Annalunkus. Now that we're friends, I wonder if you have anything to eat on board."

"Yes." She went to a cupboard. She served Matt something that was new to him, tasting like dopples, only sweeter. He drank a cool liquid from a cup. Annalunkus ate and drank, too.

She didn't do much talking. Matt guessed she was upset about running away. They had traveled quite some time, when Annalunkus suddenly cried out.

"There it is! There's Bolunkus!"

It was just a speck in the distance. She took the helm from Matt and steered toward her home. As they got closer, Matt saw that the planet was made up of mountains and of a liquid that covered the low areas. When they circled for a landing, he saw that the liquid was everywhere, even covering the spaceport. Annalunkus brought the scooter down and it splashed to a stop. The liquid was water, which can be found on some planets in the galaxy, especially on Earth, which is where Matt first came across it.

"Now what do we do?" he asked. "I can't swim."

Annalunkus was picking things up and packing them in a small carribag. "You wade, just like us Bolunkans. It's only up to your knees in most places. That's why we never wear anything on our feet. Come on."

Annalunkus opened the hatch and they climbed out onto the watery field. They splashed across it toward the main building of the spaceport. When they got inside Matt found the floor covered with water. The Bolunkans who worked there didn't seem to mind. They sat at desks or stood at counters, going about their business with water lapping at their bare ankles.

At a closed gate, Annalunkus said, "Now, don't you worry, Matthew. They'll treat you right here. Just say you want to make a call to the Moon and rent a spaceship."

The gate opened and she went through. When Matt tried to follow, the gate shut and he was grabbed roughly from behind and pushed into a separate room

73

"I didn't do anything!"

before he had a chance to say good-bye to the girl. One end of a long gadget gripped him tightly around the neck. The other was held by a Bolunkan in a green uniform that went down to his knees. On his head was a hat with a high, rounded crown. He had a large nose and smiled happily. His badge probably said what his job was, but it was in Bolunkan and Matt couldn't read it. He soon found out when the fellow spoke.

"I'm the Chief Punstable of Bolunkus. You're under arrest."

"Under arrest?" Matt echoed. "I didn't do anything."

"Certainly not," the Chief Punstable cackled. "That's why you need a rest."

9. The Riddle

They didn't treat Matt as nicely as Annalunkus had said they would. The Chief Punstable pulled Matt outside of the building where an open vehicle was parked. It floated on the water and seemed to have a rocket engine.

"Into the sloshmobile," his captor ordered Matt. They both got into the back seat. Another punstable sat behind the wheel and drove. Matt was still held by the neckcuff. He got no place trying to talk to the Chief Punstable about chartering a spaceship, or making an interspatial call to the Moon. The punstables just joked and laughed at everything. So Matt tried to relax and think of his next move.

The sloshmobile went quickly away from the spaceport and out into the countryside. Bolunkus had a water problem, that was sure. They passed a few inhabitants wading through the stuff. In some places it was up to their necks, but mostly around ankles or knees. Some houses were built in the water, and Matt noticed that the people who lived there went in and out the second-floor windows. Most of the homes were made of smooth stone and seemed to be on the dry, steep sides of the mountains. The sloshmobile kept to the low areas, though, and took Matt some distance from the spaceport. Then they came to a large hill where there were a lot of red plants growing, most of them higher than you could reach. Behind the plants, there was a building that looked like a palace. The driver drove right onto the island, and Matt saw that the sloshmobile also had wheels. At the main entrance to the palace, the Chief Punstable led Matt out of the vehicle and inside. The floors were dry, thank goodness, although Matt's feet squished inside his boots. The guards let them pass, and Matt was taken through several halls until they came to one larger than all the rest. It had a high ceiling, a balcony running all around, and a throne at one end. Then there was a shout, "All honor to the Great Klunkus!"

A group of Bolunkans dressed in fancy green robes stood at both sides of the throne. The Chief Punstable took off the neckcuff and pushed Matt out in front.

From behind the tapestry stepped a very tall Bolunkan. His green robe was decorated with fine frills. He climbed to the throne, sat down, and thumped the floor with a golden scepter he held in one hand. The Bolunkans, who had bowed, stood up straight. Matt just stared at the fellow.

The Bolunkan ruler spoke in a deep voice. "You, newcomer, do you not bow to the Great Klunkus?"

Matt decided to bluff it. "I bow to no one. It's not my scene."

Bolunkans gasped. One must not speak to the Great Klunkus like that. The Chief Punstable, afraid he might be blamed for Matt's behavior, grinned and said, "If that's not your scene, then you'll not be seen."

The Great Klunkus guffawed. "Nicely said, Chief Punstable." He looked sternly at Matt. "You would do well to show more respect for me, the beloved leader of Bolunkus. But you are a foreigner, so you shall be forgiven. Where are you from?"

"I was captured by pirates and stranded in space. I am Commander Looney of the Space Navy of the Moon. That's another planet."

"But he didn't plan it," chuckled the Chief Punstable.

At this everyone broke into laughter, including Klunkus. "Ah, Chief Punstable," he chortled, "what is your side of the story?"

At this everyone broke into laughter . . .

"My side, Your Great Klunkus, is the outside, except when it's the inside."

"That was well put," the ruler smiled.

"Well, if a well is to be put, it is well to put it well, for a well-put well does well."

Now everyone was in stitches at the Chief Punstable's jokes. These people are nuts, Matt decided, but he had to have their help, so he tried to laugh too. When they had calmed down, Klunkus spoke.

"Pirates, you say? Why, I can't believe that."

"But it's true," Matt insisted. "A great spaceship manned by wicked buccaneers and led by a Captain Morgus."

"Morgus? Morgus?" Klunkus scratched his chin. "I wonder if he's any relation to the big businessman of the same name."

"Just watch out for him, that's all I have to say," Matt warned.

"And you wish to call your Moon to bring out the Space Navy to capture this Morgus? And you're a commander in the Navy? A young fellow like you?"

"Yes, yes," Matt replied eagerly, seeing some real hope at last. "This is my uniform." Actually, Matt was wearing work clothes, which didn't have all the fancy braid on them. And his boots were filled with water. So probably it was hard for a non-Moonster to believe Matt's story.

"Let's take our time," Klunkus said. "Sit here beside me and we'll talk about it."

"But, Klunkus—Your *Great* Klunkus—" Matt said, "I can't wait for—"

"Take your time," the ruler repeated sternly.

The Chief Punstable spoke. "If you don't take time, time will take you." He threatened Matt with the neckcuff.

So Matt had to sit in a chair next to Klunkus, who clapped his hands, ordering servants to bring food and drink. At the same time jugglers, dancers, musicians, and other performers put on their acts. Every wasted moonit meant that the *Feebey* was that much further away from being rescued, Matt thought sadly. He ate and drank something, for he was hungry and thirsty, but all the while he was planning his next move.

The Great Klunkus seemed quite interested in the Moon, making Matt tell him about its population, its business, and its wealth. At one time he called on the Royal Astronomus to find out exactly how far away the Moon was from Bolunkus.

During this talk, Matt found out one more peculiar thing about Bolunkus. He had said something about the history of the Moon.

"That's something we don't have to worry about here," Klunkus declared. "History."

"Why not?"

"I don't believe in history," Klunkus said. "It causes too much trouble. I passed a law that all history books should be thrown out. And now the shelves are filled with books telling the future instead. That's much more important for the people to learn."

"The future?" Matt was really confused. "How can you have books telling the future?"

"There are no more historians. There are futurians. They get together and decide what's going to happen. Then they write books about it and teach it in the schools."

"And it happens?"

"Always," Klunkus said proudly.

These people are nuttier than a mooncake, Matt told himself. But maybe this was a way out for him. "Tell me, Klunkus, what do the books say will happen to me?"

"Oh, I'm not a very good student," the ruler smiled, "and I don't often remember tomorrow's lesson. But I can look it up for you." He clapped his hands and a servant brought him a thick, bound manuscript. "My Royal Futurian, who is never wrong, has already written the story of the rest of the day's events. Let me see." He went through the pages. "Ah, yes, here it is. *Foreigner lands on Bolunkus,* and so on. Why, it says you will ask me a riddle. That's fine. I'm crazy about riddles."

You're crazy all right, Matt agreed to himself. He put on a look of astonishment. "Why, that's amazing, Your Great Klunkus. That's exactly what I was going to do." Matt racked his brains for a good riddle.

Klunkus was very excited. "I knew it! Just as the Royal Futurian predicted. Go ahead, try me."

"All right. What is it that thrives in winter, dies in summer, and grows upside down?"

"Ah-hah," Klunkus said, leaning back, looking at the ceiling and twiddling his thumbs. "Thrives in winter —hmm—let's see."

While he struggled with it, Matt watched the entertainers and planned his next move. After a while, Klunkus shook his head and said, "I give up. What is it?"

Matt stared right into the eyes of the Great Klunkus, and replied, "I'll tell you, on one condition."

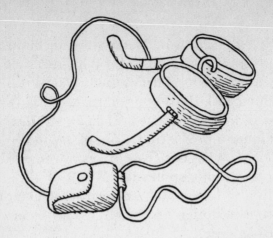

10. The Future Looks Bad

Klunkus's eyes narrowed. "No one makes conditions for the Great Klunkus, young Moonster. What did you have in mind?"

"That I be allowed to contact the Moon, and then to charter a spaceship and leave Bolunkus."

The Bolunkan ruler nodded impatiently. "Certainly. I hereby grant you permission. Now, what's the answer?" He leaned toward Matt expectantly.

Matt was suspicious. It seemed much too easy. He decided to stall for time.

"Tell me, Klunkus," he said, "if your futurians know all that is going to happen, why can't they give you the answer to my riddle?"

The dark face of Klunkus looked sad. "That is

where they fail. People who write the future have no sense of humor. A joke is funny only if it's a surprise. And nothing surprises a futurian anymore. Would you like to see for yourself?" He held out the book.

"I can't read Bolunkan."

But Klunkus set the book in Matt's lap and handed him a pair of glasses. "We are not that backward, Moonster. Here, put these on." Matt did so, and found himself looking through thick, red spectacles. Right away the Bolunkan words made sense to him.

The book was entitled *The History of Tomorrow Written Yesterday by the Royal Futurian of Bolunkus and His Staff*. Sure enough, it told about Matt's being arrested at the spaceport and being brought to the palace. Then it read:

And then it shall be, that the stranger called Moonster will tell a riddle to The Great Klunkus, our beloved leader.

Matt was really impressed. Was it some sort of mind-reading trick?

"I've never seen anything like this. How do they do it?" he asked the Bolunkan ruler.

Klunkus smiled proudly and began telling Matt how smart the Royal Futurian was. He said there was a secret room in the palace where the futurians decided what was going to happen on Bolunkus, and where they wrote the books. While Klunkus was boasting,

Matt felt a hot chill run up and down his back.

Matt turned the page and began reading some more from *The History of Tomorrow:*

Whereupon our beloved Klunkus will be friendly with the Moonster, and the Moonster will tell the answer to the riddle. Klunkus will laugh. He shall then order the stranger from outer space to be sent to prison where he will stay until further notice and—

Matt felt a hot chill run up and down his back. So that's what the old swindler was up to! He had no intention of keeping any promise he made, and Matt would probably be stuck on Bolunkus the rest of his life. Matt slowly looked up and smiled at Klunkus, who was so busy talking he hadn't noticed what Matt had done.

Now's the time for action, Matt realized. He slowly took off the spectacles and tucked them in a pocket. He reached for his solar gun and quietly stood up. Then suddenly he grabbed Klunkus from behind.

"Stand back!" he shouted at the others. There were a few screams, but they mostly moved back. Except for one, a punstable on guard who rushed toward the throne. Matt quickly fired a solar pellet his way and the brave but foolish Bolunkan fell to the floor, unconscious, his ears steaming. He would recover in a few hours, but the Bolunkans didn't know that—they thought he was dead. They looked in horror at the body.

But Matt had put himself in a dangerous spot. He had fired the last of his ammunition. Why, oh why hadn't he loaded his gun when he had the chance? he asked himself. He would have to bluff it. At least, none of the Bolunkans knew he held an empty solar gun. He jammed it into his prisoner's back.

"If you value your life, Klunkus," Matt declared, "you will give orders to have a spaceship ready for me to fly to the Moon. And you're coming with me to the spaceport."

"Ouch, you're hurting me," Klunkus said. "You can't do this. It's a waste of time. The futurians—"

"Phooey on the futurians," Matt interrupted. "I come from another planet, and I can change the course of my own future. Now, let's go."

"All right, all right. Chief Punstable! Order a ship to be ready for a journey to the Moon! Then take us to the spaceport in your sloshmobile."

"Yes, Your Royal Klunkus." The Chief Punstable hurried off to obey.

Matt started walking his prisoner out of the room, the Bolunkans stepping out of the way and following at a distance. His fine sense of direction led Matt back the way he had come, and he soon reached the entrance hall. He gripped the Great Klunkus firmly and pushed the gun into his back.

"No funny business, now," he ordered, and started

toward the main door. He could see the Chief Punstable outside waiting beside his car. I'll make it, Matt thought. But something startled him. The Bolunkans behind him began a disturbance. He quickly turned. Then he heard a voice cry, "It's the Princess!"

From the other side of the hall, a figure approached. It was a young Bolunkan girl, with long red hair and slim body, dressed in a fine green robe. Matt's jaw dropped in surprise as he recognized her. The runaway, Annalunkus!

She was just as surprised as he. "The Moon boy! What are you doing with Daddy?" she demanded, and walked closer.

"Keep away, daughter," Klunkus said. "This person is dangerous. He just shot one of us."

She hesitated a moonit, then she smiled and walked closer, step by step. Matt pointed the gun at her. Why was she so sure of herself, he wondered.

"I'll shoot!" he yelled, hoping to scare her.

"He will!" Klunkus warned.

"I don't think so," she smiled. She put out her hand. "Here, give me that." She put her hand on the barrel of the gun and gently took it from Matt's grasp. His arms dropped to his sides. Punstables rushed forward and snapped a neckcuff on him.

"Ah," the Great Klunkus sighed. "You're a brave girl, Annalunkus."

Matt looked at her. "Why did you do that?"

She laughed. "I'm not so brave. Remember? You told me when we met, your gun only had one bullet in it. I was just hoping it was empty. Besides, you wouldn't shoot a nice girl like me, would you?"

I'll never know, Matt thought.

"Take him to prison," Klunkus ordered, "just as it is written in the book." And they led Commander Matthew Looney away.

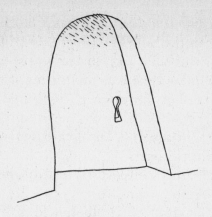

11. A Surprise Visit

Once again Matt went for a ride in the sloshmobile. The Chief Punstable kept a tight grip on the neckcuff, while the machine squished away from the palace and across the damp Bolunkan countryside.

"I am mad and sad that you have been bad, my lad," the officer said.

Matt was mad, too, at everybody and everything. At himself for getting into such a fix. At that Annalunkus girl. She was the reason he was on this planet. He should have just steered the space scooter straight for the Moon, and maybe the *Feebey* would have been rescued by now.

Pretty soon they came to another one of those hilly islands that stuck up out of the water. The driver stopped at a gate, and Matt saw that it blocked the way into the side of the hill. The Chief Punstable got Matt out of the sloshmobile and led him to the entrance. A punstable unlocked the gate and swung it open.

"I am here to cell a prisoner," the Chief Punstable said with a grin.

"To sell a prisoner?" The guard looked puzzled. "We don't buy prisoners."

The Chief's grin vanished. "To CELL him! *CELL!* Get it, you dumb bunkus?"

"Oh, yes, sir. Ha-ha." He took hold of Matt by the neckcuff. The Chief Punstable got into the sloshmobile and was driven away. The guard led Matt into a dim tunnel that went deep into the mountain. After a while they came out into a big cave lit up by sulphur bulbs in the walls and ceiling. All around the cave were smaller caves in which the prisoners lived. There were no windows and no bars. The only way in or out seemed to be through the tunnel. The guard took off the neckcuff and left Matt standing there. As he started to go, Matt grabbed him.

"Wait a moonit," he demanded. "What am I here for? How long before I get out?"

The guard looked surprised. "Those are silly questions. My job is to keep the gate locked, that's all. Besides, I don't even know who you are." He hurried away through the tunnel.

Matt felt helpless. He looked around. A few other prisoners were standing in the main cave, and in the smaller rooms he could see others. Matt didn't know which cell he was supposed to be in, so he started looking for an empty one. He wanted a place to rest and think. The Bolunkans watched him, knowing from his looks that he was not one of them, but no one spoke to him until he heard a voice from one of the cells.

"Hello. Where did you come from?"

And that was how Matt met Zinkus, the first Bolunkan he ever got to know very well. Like the others, he was tall and thin, dressed in a green robe and with bare feet. But he seemed smarter than any of the others. He was a schoolteacher.

"And that's why I'm in prison," he told Matt.

"But that's terrible," the Moonster said. "They shouldn't put teachers in prison."

"Ah, but I taught history, and that's against the law now."

Through Zinkus, Matt met a few other prisoners. Most of them were there because they had done something to displease the Great Klunkus, like teaching history, or not bowing to him. When Matt told them he was from the Moon, hardly anyone had heard of the place, except for a few of the history teachers. But he didn't care. What he was really interested in was a way

"The Hotheads are the last hope of Bolunkans."

to escape, and he was overjoyed to find that Zinkus had the same idea. Matt's Bolunkan friend was the leader of the Hotheads, prisoners who planned to break out and take over the government.

"The Hotheads are the last hope of Bolunkus," the schoolteacher told Matt. "We shall overthrow Klunkus, and put his punstables in jail. It won't be easy, but we will win."

"I'm with you, friend," Matt said.

"Thanks, Looney," Zinkus replied. "We can use you."

He took Matt to a faraway part of the cave. The Hotheads had somehow gotten shoves and pickels, and were digging an escape tunnel.

"When we break through here, it'll all be over," Zinkus said proudly.

But the more Matt learned about the Hotheads, the more discouraged he got. The tunnel, he learned, was a long way from finished. When the Hotheads had meetings, they argued about their plans. Some wanted to get a spaceship and bomb the palace. Others wanted to march on the palace, even though they had no weapons. Others said they should print an underground newspaper and call for the Bolunkan people to rise up. Or kidnap Annalunkus. Or burn the palace. And so on. The only thing they could agree on was that they hated prison, mainly because it was dry.

Bolunkans are happiest when they are standing in water, Matt found out.

As life in the prison dragged on, the unhappy Moonster got more gloomy about his chances of getting away. When he wasn't helping to dig the tunnel, he explored the cave. It stretched quite a distance under the mountain, but every passage came to a dead end. Even if there were another way out, what good would it do him? He couldn't find his way around Bolunkus without help. That's why he needed the Hotheads. But the way they were going, things didn't look hopeful. Even when they did escape, just how were they going to win a revolution, without weapons and without plans?

Matt tried to talk with the punstable who brought the food cart, but that was no use. All in all, the picture looked very bad. Not only did Matt see no hope for rescuing the *Feebey*, but he didn't even see how he himself would ever be free. And he realized that he was now in the worst predicament of his whole life, with no real hope of getting out of it.

Then one day—or night, who could tell?—an amazing event changed everything. Matt woke up feeling low, and just lay there on his rocky bunk not wanting to get up. After all, there was no place to go. Zinkus entered the tiny cell.

"They've brought a new prisoner in. Come and see."

"Just what we need," Matt replied sourly. "Why should I be interested?"

"He's not a Bolunkan. I haven't talked to him, but he might be—I can't tell for sure—a Moonster."

"That's impossible, Zinkus."

But Matt was curious enough to follow Zinkus across the floor of the central cave to the main door, where a group of prisoners were huddled around the newcomer. Matt pushed his way through and got the surprise of his life. He could hardly believe his eyes.

"Mister Bones!"

For indeed it was he. The old space salt's jaw dropped when he saw his commander. "Matt! Matt Looney! What in starnation be *you* doin' here?"

"What about *you?* How did you get here?" Matt responded.

The two Moonsters told their stories. Matt quickly explained his side, and then heard from Mr. Bones. It was simple enough. After making Matt walk the plank, Captain Morgus flew around the galaxy looking for more spaceships to capture. Finding none, he had decided to return home with the *Feebey* and its passengers as prisoners.

"You mean Captain Morgus is from Bolunkus?" Matt asked in astonishment.

Mr. Bones nodded.

"And where are the others?"

"They be on the way," Mr. Bones said. "Right now they be searched by a funny galoot with a round hat on his head. He be lookin' for guns. 'Any rockets in your pockets?' he asked me."

"That's the Chief Punstable."

The Bolunkans listened impatiently to the conversation. Of course, as it was in Moon language, they couldn't understand a word. Zinkus jiggled Matt's elbow and asked what it was all about.

Matt translated everything into Bolunkan, and then added, "You never told me Captain Morgus was a Bolunkan."

"Why, I never thought it could be the same person," Zinkus said. "The only Morgus I know of here is a big businessman, and president of the Bolunkan Chamber of Commerce."

"It's big business, all right. He's got our moonship with all its valuable supplies," Matt said. "All my people are captured. And you Hotheads are still digging that measly tunnel."

Zinkus looked hurt. "Well, if you have a better idea, let's hear it."

Matt didn't, so he turned to Mr. Bones again. "Tell me, are the Moonsters well?"

"They be well enough, Commander, considerin' what's happened. And one of 'em is better 'n the rest."

"Who?"

"Hector Hornblower. He warn't taken prisoner."

"No? Why not?"

"He got real friendly with Morgus. Last I heered he was goin' to meet the top Bolunkan mucky-muck, named Klunkus, or something like that."

"Oh!" Matt clenched his fists. "Wait till I get my hands on that traitor Hector!"

"And," Mr. Bones added, "he's livin' at the palace!"

12. Hector Has a Problem

The palace rang with laughter. The Great Klunkus sat at the head of a long table in the big dining hall. Flags and fine tapestries hung upon the walls. Blazing logs filled the fireplaces. Magicians and dancers performed, while court jesters did somersaults and tricks. Servants hurried back and forth, carrying platters of food. Seated at the table were the Bolunkan pirates. Their leader, Captain Morgus, sat on one side of Klunkus, who was patting him on the back.

"Great work, Morgus. We'll all be rich if you keep it up. A few more prizes like the *Feebey* and we can retire to the country and take it easy."

"Ho, ho, ho!" Morgus roared happily. "It sure beats working for the Chamber of Commerce, I tell you."

On the other side of Klunkus sat a non-Bolunkan, who joined in the fun. It was none other than Hector Hornblower. And he was really enjoying himself. Klunkus banged his tankard on the table and shouted for silence.

"Fellow Bolunkans," he declared, "a toast to our good friend, the Moonster Hornblower. We owe him much, but especially this marvelous beverage—*firmamented canal juice*—the best tasting stuff I ever did swallow!"

The pirates leaped to their feet. Their cheers shook the building. "To Hornblower!" Then each gulped from his drinking mug.

"More vittles!" Klunkus ordered, sending the servants to the kitchen for food. He put an arm around Hector's shoulders. "You're a great fellow, even though you are from the Moon. I don't think much of your friend, though, the one who tried to kidnap me."

Hector smiled. "Looney? No friend of mine, Your Royal Klunkus."

"Ho, ho, ho!" Captain Morgus roared. "Spoken like a true scalawag. Yes, sir, we're really going to get along fine. And when you finish unloading that moonship, we've got a bigger and better job for you. Right, Klunkus?"

"Right!" Klunkus rubbed his hands together. "A very special space trip that you're really going to enjoy.

Yes, we're going to make a great team. After we get the accounting all straightened out, and send those Moonsters to where they won't bother us anymore, I'll settle you down in a castle of your own. I want you to meet my daughter. She's the prettiest thing you'll ever see, Hornblower. How would you like to be Chief Punstable? Say, this canal juice really makes a person talk, doesn't it?"

"Anything I can do for your nice planet would be my pleasure," Hector smiled.

That night the Moonster lay in a soft bed in a fine room in the palace. Who would want to live on Hercules, or even back on the Moon, when there was a deal like this to be had? Starting at the top, a job as Chief Punstable, a castle. He could hardly wait to meet the Princess. He fell asleep and dreamed of a marvelous life on Bolunkus.

But it wasn't all play for Hector Hornblower. The Great Klunkus had given the Moonster the job of making a record of the contents of the moonship. Its hold was packed with goods that no Bolunkan would know what to do with, having never seen them before. Hector's job was to explain, translate directions, etc. He was also supposed to help dismantle the moonship so its parts could be used. He was getting instructions in the throne room one morning when the Chief Punstable arrived, bowing low. The badges on his uni-

*"Anything I can do for your nice planet
would be my pleasure."*

form rattled, and his big hat fell off his head and rolled across the floor.

"Your Royal Klunkus," he announced, "the Moonsters are in the dungeon's gloomy room, doomed in the tomb, I presume."

"Good work, Punstable. You may leave."

"I zoom," the Chief Punstable said, flapping his arms as he left.

"Is that the job you offered me?" Hector asked. "Do I really have to wear that uniform, and talk funny like that?"

"Certainly. And you'll be very good at it, too. Right now, before you leave for the day's work, I want you to meet my daughter." Klunkus clapped his hands, the heavy curtains behind the throne parted, and Annalunkus stepped forward. Hector looked at her and smiled. She was taller than he was, and she was very thin. And her hair was red. Well, it was better than nothing. He bowed.

"Hornblower," her father said, "this is Princess Annalunkus. Daughter, this is Prince Hector of Moon, your betrothed." That "prince" was a little lie that Hector had told.

Annalunkus looked suspicious.

"My *what*, Daddy?"

"Your betrothed, the man you will some day marry."

"Marry? Him? He's not even a Bolunkan. And he's so short and pale."

"There are no princes on Bolunkus, daughter. And every time my men bring you a blueblood, you say he's too this, or too that."

"I don't want to marry anybody!" cried Annalunkus. "I'm too young. And, anyway, if I do, it will be some nice Bolunkan fellow, not someone your pirates picked out of the Universe!" She stormed from the hall.

"Don't mind her," Klunkus reassured Hector. "She'll change her mind. And now you'd better get yourself down to the spaceport and go to work on the moonship."

"Yes, sir."

"And one more thing, Hector. I have decided to have another celebration tonight, so bring back a supply of that marvelous canal juice."

The Great Klunkus thereupon dismissed the court. He made his way alone to a small doorway, and up a narrow, winding staircase. Round and round he went, finally reaching an iron door. He knocked, identified himself, and was admitted. He was inside a large library, except that the shelves had very few books upon them. At desks sat Bolunkans who wrote in notebooks. They were the futurians, busy recording the history of events-to-be. The Royal Futurian greeted his sovereign with a grin.

"Good day, Your Royal Klunkus. Would you like to know what is about to happen?"

"Not now, Futurian. I am more interested in our big project, you know what I mean?"

"Certainly. Right over here."

They moved across the room to one of the desks. An old man with a long beard was at work there. He handed his notebook to the Great Klunkus. The title on the cover was: *Chapter Forty-four: How the Bolunkan Pirates Invaded the Moon.* Klunkus turned the pages slowly.

"I would especially like to know," he said, "how our brave buccaneers found their way to such a distant place, and how they managed to approach the Moon without alarming its inhabitants."

"Well, sir," cackled the old fellow, "we can have it come out any way you please. But I have had a lot of experience with the future, and I like the idea of a traitorous Moonster. You will bribe him, and he will turn against his own people."

That pleased Klunkus. He asked if the traitor's name could be Hornblower. The old futurian said it could be, and began writing it all down in Chapter Forty-four of *The History of Tomorrow.* Later, when the chapter was completed, Klunkus broke the news to Hector that he was going to lead a band of pirates against his old home planet. The Moonster was so softened up by the happy life on Bolunkus and promises of things to come, that he didn't seem to mind. He spent his days puttering around the moon-ship, making an accounting of its contents. When he was through work, he would be driven back to the palace by his punstable chauffeur. He never had a chance to talk to Annalunkus, because she would scurry away whenever she saw him. Usually there was a big party, with lots of food and drink, and Hector would have a good time there.

One night he was in his regular seat next to Klunkus, when the Bolunkan ruler thumped the table with his big tankard and called, "More canal juice!"

A servant brought a pitcher and poured a few drops into the tankard. The pitcher was empty.

"More! More!" Klunkus demanded.

"Begging Your Klunkus's pardon," the waiter said, "that's all there is."

"Get some in the kitchen, then."

"There is no more in the kitchen, Your Royal Klunkus."

"What is the meaning of this, Hornblower?" the monarch asked. "How can we have a party without canal juice?"

"You drink it too fast. I brought four juggoons back with me tonight, and you've finished them already."

But Klunkus had to have more canal juice. He

sent Hector to the spaceport to fetch a fresh supply. Now, the reason Hector had brought only four juggoons to the palace was that there was no more. He had been afraid to say so. His only hope was that somewhere on the *Feebey* was some firmamented canal juice that he had overlooked. The chances of that were slim. With the Great Klunkus losing his temper, Hector made one more search. While his chauffeur waited, he rummaged through the galley, the hold, and the staterooms.

What made him mad was that there was plenty of canal juice, both powdered and liquid, because it was a favorite drink of Moonsters. But none of it was firmamented. Hector had no idea how to change the ordinary stuff into the bubbly beverage that tasted so delightful. That had to be done at a moonshinery. He wished now that he hadn't drunk so much of it himself, for there would have been more for Klunkus. He finally gave up looking and returned to the palace with the sad news.

Hector had been gone quite a while, and when he entered the big dining hall, it was almost empty. The Great Klunkus was still at the head of the table.

"Well, it's about time," he bellowed. "Look! All my guests have gone home because we ran out of canal juice. Well, at least I can have a nightcap. Fill my tankard."

Hector tried to smile. "Your Royal Klunkus, sir. I regret to inform you that—um—all the canal juice has been used up. It's all gone."

"All the—used up—gone? Are you sure?"

"Quite."

Klunkus looked as if he were about to weep. He stared at his empty tankard. Then he turned to Hector in anger.

"Moonster," he declared, shaking the empty tankard in his face, "you get yourself another supply of canal juice, and soon, or you'll find yourself in the deepest dungeon you ever saw, prince or no prince. The Great Klunkus has spoken." He stomped out of the hall.

That night Hector tossed and turned in his big bed. All his fancy dreams would turn to dust unless he could satisfy Klunkus. He finally figured out what to do to save his skin. But there was one hitch to the scheme— and it was a big one: it required the help of Matthew Looney, his enemy.

13. A Daring Plan

Prison life was a little bit easier on Matt, now that the Moonsters were there with him. At least they were safe and sound, and not floating out in space without food or fuel. Vice-Chairman Heckity and the others had, of course, been surprised and happy to find young Commander Looney in the cave. Stories were exchanged, and Matt introduced Zinkus and the Hotheads to the Moonsters.

It didn't take long, though, for everyone to feel pretty blue about the fix they were in. Matt was down in the dumps himself, but he couldn't let himself show it.

"Cheer up," he told the others. "We'll get out of this mess somehow."

He knew that the first thing was to get everyone busy, to take their minds off their problems. Work crews were organized to help dig the escape tunnel. Classes were held for youngsters, and some adults, too. In one section of the large cave, a cleaning and repair service was opened up to handle clothing. Although the Bolunkans supplied plenty of food, most of it was stuff never seen on the Moon, and Moonsters didn't like it so much. So Wondervon Brown, chef of the *Feebey,* set up a kitchen, where he cooked the Bolunkan food over again to make it taste familiar. He also used some supplies he had brought from the moonship. One time Matt and Zinkus were having a snack together. The Moonster bit into a cake.

"Mmmm, this is good. I wonder what it is."

Zinkus tasted one. "It seems to be made of yokel root. Your man has added something special to it."

From behind the counter, Wondervon Brown watched. "Is good, yah?" he smiled.

The two agreed it was, and Brown went back to stirring a pot of mashed blunkoes.

"He's excellent," Matt told Zinkus. "He wrote a book called *Cosmic Cookery* that became a best seller back home. It tells you how to make dishes out of strange foods you find in space. Like starflakes, for instance, or nebbles, which most folks think can't be eaten."

"Too bad he didn't write a book on how to escape from caves," Zinkus grumbled.

Matt, Heckity, Zinkus, and the Hotheads held many meetings trying to figure out what to do. Matt had searched every corner of the cave and found that there were no secret exits. One of the Hotheads wanted everyone to charge the gate and break through. That idea was turned down as being too dangerous for women and children. Zinkus wanted one of the small Moonsters to hide in the food cart, and smuggle himself out that way. But what would he do when he got out there? Lots of schemes were thought of and dropped, for one reason or another.

At one of these meetings they were sitting glumly around the big stone table in the conference cave. A Moonster came with a message. Commander Looney was wanted at the gate. Hector Hornblower was there to see him.

Hector! Matt gritted his teeth, clenched his fists, and growled, "That rat! Tell him to go back to his palace and leave us alone." The messenger turned to leave.

"Wait," Zinkus said. "Perhaps you should talk to him. You might find out something helpful."

"I wouldn't be able to control myself."

"Then send someone else."

Matt agreed that Zinkus was probably right, so Vice-

Chairman Heckity was sent in his place. It seemed that he was gone for a long time, for they were curious and impatient to know what brought the traitor Hornblower to the underground prison of his fellow Moonsters. Finally, Heckity returned. He fell into his chair, shaking his head in puzzlement. "I can't believe it."

"Can't believe what? Out with it, fellow," Matt insisted.

Heckity then told the strange story. Hector Hornblower badly wanted a supply of firmamented canal juice for the Great Klunkus. There was plenty of the undistilled stuff to be had, but someone who knew the recipe was needed to treat it. The Great Klunkus and his pirate crews had fallen in love with the bubbly drink, and they had to have more. No telling what terrible revenge they would seek if they didn't get some. Hector was almost in tears.

Matt snorted. "Why should we do them a favor like that?"

"Hector says he'll make a deal," Heckity continued. "He'll see that we are rewarded."

"Well, that's more like it," Matt smiled. "Refuel our ship and we'll be on our way."

"Nothing like that," the vice-chairman said.

"Then what do we get in return?"

"Well, he thinks he can talk Klunkus into moving us to a nicer prison."

"I've got it!"

"Ridiculous!" Matt cried out. "What kind of deal is that?"

"Klunkus can't be trusted, anyway," Zinkus declared.

The commander leaned his elbows on the stone table and rested his chin in his hands. No one spoke, for the picture looked grim, indeed, if this was the kind of "deal" that Hector and Klunkus were going to offer. Then Matt began to wonder. Maybe the canal juice shortage could be turned into an advantage for the Moonsters. Another one of his clever schemes formed in his brain. He leaped to his feet with a shout.

"I've got it!"

"What is it?" the startled group asked.

"We are going to help Hector and Klunkus, that's what. Now, listen carefully. Here's my plan. Vice-Chairman, you report to Hector that we shall distill the juice for him, in return for moving us to a nicer prison. The distilling machine is in the *Feebey*, so our distiller will have to do the job there. Tell Hector to send a sloshtruck to the gate, with plenty of empty juggoons, to pick up our man and take him to the spaceship."

Heckity hurried off to follow his instructions.

"And now, as you can see," Matt continued, "in this manner we shall smuggle one of our people outside."

"But who?" someone asked. "No one in our group knows anything about distilling canal juice."

"Oh, yes, Wondervon Brown knows how. He once worked in a moonshinery in Crater Copernicus back home."

"But," Zinkus inquired, "what good will it do us to have your cook shut up in a spaceship running a distillery? He makes good meals, but otherwise he is very dumb, and hardly the type of person we can expect to get us out of the fix we're in."

"Ah, but it won't be our cook. It will be me, dressed up as Wondervon Brown. That will give me the chance to carry out my plan, which will result in the overthrow of Klunkus and all his followers!"

14. Matt's Disguise

There wasn't much time to prepare. Hector was in a hurry. The truck with its juggoons would be at the prison gate soon. First Matt called upon Wondervon Brown in the kitchen.

"Yah, Commander, can I help you?"

"Brown, I need some information. You used to work in a moonshinery, as I understand it."

"Yah."

"Could you brew canal juice now, if you had to?"

"Oh, no, Commander. Dot would be hard to do."

"Why?"

"I need big tanks, und pipes, und hot fires, und tings like popper sauce, mushmoons, und lots of puckles. I don't have none of dose tings here."

"But didn't we bring such supplies with us when we left home?" Matt asked.

Brown thought a moonit. "Oh, yah, I suppose. But, in der *Feebey*"—he shrugged his big shoulders—"dey might as well be on der Moon."

Matt moved closer to the big fellow and spoke quietly. "Brown, I am going to the spaceship to make some firmamented canal juice. I haven't time to give you the whole story, but believe me, it's for the good of us all. Now, I want you to tell me how to make the stuff."

"How you get dere? What you use for der big tanks, und pipes, und hot fires?"

"Don't you worry about that. I've got it figured out. Now, you just tell me the recipe, slowly, while I write it down."

The cook chuckled. "Ock, dere's no need for dot, mine little friend. It's all written down."

Matt was surprised. "How come?"

Brown reached under the counter and pulled out a book. "It's all here, in der best seller, *Cosmic Cookery*." He flipped the pages. "Yah, here it is. Page eighty-eight. Look, dere's even a picture of a moonshinery, und a drawing of der way it works."

The Space Commander could hardly believe it. "Why, that's marvelous!" he cried, reaching for the book. "I'll take that with me."

118

Brown closed the book and held it tightly. "Dot's fourteen rubbles, plus tax."

"What? You mean you're going to charge me? At a time like this?"

"You don't tink I make mooney on mine books by giving dem away, do you?"

"Oh, all right," Matt said, counting out the bills. "Here. But there's no tax on Bolunkus, and I'm not paying it."

"Dot's all right." Brown grabbed the fourteen rubbles.

"Now, there's one more thing, Brown."

The cook smiled. "Sure, you want me to autograph der book."

"Lend me your hat and apron."

The big fellow jumped back. "Hat und apron? You out of der noodle? No chef ever gives up dose."

Trying to keep calm, Matt explained that he was going to slip out of the cave dressed as a cook who knew how to make canal juice. Brown was even more upset.

"You cannot do dot! Me, I Wondervon Brown. You, you Matthew Looney. I never let you be me, or me be you. Dot's final." He turned away.

"Brown! I haven't time to argue with you. Turn over your uniform. That's an order."

Brown slowly took off the apron and chef's cap, looking as though he were about to cry. Matt took the things, and picking up a big ladle, left in a rush. He was going to ask Brown to come along to help with the disguise, but he thought the stubborn guy would be more trouble than he was worth.

When he got back to the conference cave, he found the others waiting nervously. Vice-Chairman Heckity had received word that the sloshtruck, with two punstables as guards, was waiting at the gate.

"Hurry!" Matt said. "I need some hair." He looked around. All the Moonsters had short hair. Then he saw Zinkus, whose long red locks fell to his shoulders. "Ah, hah! Give me the scissors. Come here, Zinkus. It's for the revolution." Almost before the tall Bolunkan knew what was happening, Matt had clipped off pieces of hair from the fellow's head. He called for glue, and told the others how to stick the hair to his face. In a jiffy Matt had a walrus mustache and side-whiskers. They stuck more to his head, so it hung down over his ears. Matt tied the apron around his waist and put on the chef's hat.

"One more thing," Heckity said. He found some old clothing and padded Matt's shoulders and waist so that he looked fat.

When they were finished Matt waved the ladle. "Yah, how do I look?"

"Perfect," Heckity said. "They'll never know."

Quickly, Matt gave instructions to Zinkus and the

When they were finished Matt waved the ladle.

Hotheads, as well as to the vice-chairman and his staff. They were to gather all able-bodied Moonsters and Bolunkans and prepare them for a raid on the palace. Matt promised that sooner or later he would be back to open the prison gate for them. He didn't have time to explain exactly how he would manage it. To tell the truth, he really didn't know. He tucked *Cosmic Cookery* under his arm, waved a farewell with the ladle, and waddled toward the gate.

Going through the gloomy passageway, Matt was a bit nervous. His fine plan could break down rather soon in two ways: one, if Hector saw through the disguise, and two, if he was unable to firmament canal juice. He was happy to find that it was dark outside, which made it a little easier to fool anyone who might be suspicious. He was even happier to find that Hector was not there to meet him. The guards were expecting a Moonster cook, and when Matt appeared they passed him through the gate without lifting an eyebrow. Two punstables snapped a neckcuff on him, put him in the truck that was parked there, and got in with him. They didn't look twice at him. Matt breathed a sigh of relief. So far, so good.

15. The Lavaberry Essence

The sloshtruck squished away from the prison and across the watery land of Bolunkus. They came to a town. Bolunkans waded through the streets, going about their business. On the other side of the town they came to the spaceport, where many ships were parked. The truck sloshed across the field. Matt saw Captain Morgus's pirate space vessel, *Adventurer of the Universe*. Next to it was Matt's beloved moonship, the *Feebey*. The truck stopped alongside.

One of the punstables remained in the truck, while the other went with Matt as he climbed into the *Feebey*. Stepping into the familiar spaceship—which he had once thought he would never see again—was a pleasant thrill for the Moonster. He paused and looked around. The Bolunkan pirates had left it in quite a mess. He hoped the ship would be in flying condition when the time came to take off. Well, that was something to worry about later. Right now—on with the canal juice.

"Let go der cuff," he told the punstable, trying to talk like Wondervon Brown. "I can't work mit dot ting around mine neck." The guard did so, and stood at the door, while Matt began work. First, he sat down and studied the cookbook. He jotted down notes. When he was ready, he went to the galley and collected the ingredients called for, such as puckles, popper sauce, mushmoons, and dried canal juice. He then carried everything down the ladder to the engine room. From his knowledge of the moonship's powerful motors, he knew he would find big tanks and pipes.

It is too complicated to explain here, but what Matt did was to drain the two largest boilers. He started the small, emergency reciprocators and cleaned their insides. He placed the ingredients in Boiler Number 1, heating them by means of the reciprocator blow-lamp. Then, bypassing the main feed lines, he forced the mixture through the small valves of the back vent, and into Boiler Number 2. This gave the canal juice the carbonation it needed, but did not spoil the flavor.

At least, that was the way Matt had it figured out. He hoped he was right. He studied the cookbook again and again as he worked. The process took a long, long, time. It wasn't easy, especially as he had to move with all that stuffing around his stomach. The engine room was filled with vapor, the hissing sound of valves, and the clanking of metal pipes as the hot stuff flowed through them. All the racket had brought the punstable to the head of the engine room ladder. He watched with interest.

Finally it came time to test. Matt had drunk firmamented canal juice only a few times in his life, and he hoped he would be able to tell if this batch was any good. He found a cup, and drew some of the hot bubbly stuff from a tap in Boiler Number 2. He blew on it to cool it, and then put his lips to it. It smelled good. It tasted good. He swallowed a little. It *was* good! He had succeeded! Probably the first time anyone in the universe had ever brewed canal juice in a spaceship engine instead of in a moonshinery. The young Space Commander was pleased with himself.

Now came the tricky part. The punstable was still watching, so Matt had to be careful. He swallowed some more and licked his lips. "Ock, das is goot." He called to the guard. "You und your pal, how about you should have a schnapps, yah?"

The fellow nodded eagerly.

"Goot. Bring der juggoons und fill dem. Den I give you."

He blew on it to cool it.

The Bolunkan left and Matt swung into action. Spread all over the floor were empty bottles and boxes. There was one small bottle that he had not opened. It had come not from the kitchen, but from the doctor's office in sick bay. Matt grabbed it and quickly read the label again:

DANGER

ESSENCE OF LAVABERRY

For severe cases
of Moononucleosis.

Habit-forming.
Mind-blowing.
Beware of Trips.

To Be Taken Only On
Advice Of Physician

He unscrewed the cap. He read the directions. It seemed that one drop of essence of lavaberry was a strong dose. It was powerful. The question was, what effect would it have if—the punstables were coming!— he jumped to the steps leading to the top of Boiler Number 2, and opened the lid. A cloud of bubbly juice splashed on him. He upended the little bottle and shook all of the essence into the firmament, closed the lid, and climbed down just in time to meet the punstables as they carried the first load of juggoons in.

"Make it snappy," one of them said. "We gotta get this stuff to the palace in time for the party."

They started filling. Matt worked the tap, while the other two carried the containers out and packed them in the back of the truck. When the last of them had been put away, the punstables returned for their reward. There was still lots of firmamented canal juice left in Boiler Number 2. Matt drew a full cup for each. He picked up his own cup and lifted it high.

"To der Great Klunkus!"

The Bolunkans broke into grins and repeated, "To the Great Klunkus!" They drank deeply. They liked it, and asked for more. Matt watched them carefully as they each drained a second cup. Nothing. His hopes fell. The next step in his scheme had depended on the essence of lavaberry. It now seemed that he couldn't count on it. But he had given up too soon. One of the punstables was quietly holding out his cup for another portion, when suddenly he gave a shriek, "Harook!"— it sounded like that to Matt—threw the cup away, leaped high in the air, and came down on hands and feet. He then began galloping around the engine room on all fours, bumping into machinery, yelling, "Harook! Harook! I'm a flippen!"

His partner watched in amazement, turned to Matt and opened his mouth to say something. No words came out, yet his mouth opened and shut and opened, biting the steamy atmosphere and gulping. He tossed his cup away, too, and began swimming a sort of breast-stroke across the deck, sliding his feet forward one after the other. He was swimming and groaning, "Rah-woo-rah-woo-rah-woo!" He sounded like some animal calling for its mother. Matt ran to a corner to get out of the way. One punstable leaping up and down, the other swimming back and forth. The tap on Boiler Number 2 dripped, and soon the two were slipping and sliding around in canal juice. They would crash against one end of the room, get up and start their acts again, bump into each other, and come down on the frothy floor in a heap, all the time yelling, "Rah-woo-rah!" and "Harook!"

Then, just as suddenly as it had begun, the performance ended. The two punstables collapsed on the deck, out cold. Matt waited. They didn't move. Wow, he thought, so that's what lavaberry essence can do to you. Some wild trip! He checked the unconscious Bolunkans. They were alive. He didn't know when they would come to, so he had to hurry. He now had a marvelous feeling of relief. For the first time since he had landed on this crazy planet, he was free. He was on his own, and it was good.

"Wait till Klunkus and his boys
get a taste of this!"

Now, for the next move. He took off Wondervon Brown's cap and apron, and pulled out all the stuffing. He rolled one of the Bolunkans over, got his uniform off, and put it on over his own clothes. It hung down to his feet, but it would have to do. He slapped the punstable hat on his head and clambered up the ladder, out of the engine room, through the spaceship and out the main hatch, locking it after him. There was the truck, loaded with juggoons of doped firmamented canal juice. He jumped into the driver's seat and started the motor.

"Oh, boy!" Matt exulted. "Wait till Klunkus and his boys get a taste of *this!*"

16. Inside the Palace

It is really amazing what a Moonster can do on Bolun-kus when wearing the uniform of a punstable. Matt still had those remarkable glasses he had gotten from Klunkus that day, and so he was able to read signs on the roads and words on the instrument panel of the truck. He drove through the city without anyone pay-ing him any attention. When he got to the royal palace island, he pressed a button marked DRY and the vehi-cle scooted right onto the land. He followed the drive-way to the rear of the palace, backed up to the kitchen door, and shouted, "Canal juice!"

Smiling servants rushed outside and began unload-ing. They barely glanced at Matt, and in the dark failed to notice anything out of the ordinary. While they lugged the heavy juggoons inside, Matt faded away into the shadows without being missed. The bubbly brew was on its way to the banquet tables. What a party Klunkus would have tonight! And now Matt was faced with a tough one: how to get the keys to the prison from the Chief Punstable.

According to the information Zinkus had given him, the Chief Punstable would probably not be at the party. He could be found either in his quarters or in the guardroom. Matt had memorized the layout. He hugged the rear wall of the building, finally coming to a heavy vine that was firmly attached. He tested it, then climbed up hand and foot. Dim lights shone from most of the windows on this side of the palace. Although he could not see within, he guessed that those rooms were probably occupied. Up and up he went. He looked down. Light from the open kitchen door fell on the figures of the servants still unloading the truck. He looked up, spotting a darkened window in the tower. He gripped the thick vine, stepped carefully, and made his way toward it. He was becoming tired. Slowly he climbed, finally getting a hand over the edge of the window, rested a moonit, and then hoisted himself inside. He lowered himself to the floor and sat there, getting back his strength.

He listened, but couldn't hear any noises that meant anything to him. Where was he? In the tower, he knew that much, and the Chief Punstable's room should be nearby. What if this was it? Slowly he got to his feet, groping in the gloom until he found a lamp. He pressed, and a sulphur bulb flashed on, flooding the room with light. This wasn't anyone's living quarters. It was a sort of library, except that the shelves held no books. There were many desks, where workers had left their papers. Matt put on his glasses. He read from the cover of a notebook on a desk: *The History of Tomorrow. Chapter Twelve: How Prison Will Be Filled and a New One Will Be Built.*

Now Matt knew where he was. The secret room where the futurians write down what will happen! The young space commander was slightly awed by his discovery. He did not believe that professors—no matter how wise they might be—could sit down and write books telling about events yet to take place. But here they were—notebooks filled with stories of the future. Did this really mean, he asked himself, that things would have to happen as written? Klunkus had already proven so, in a couple of cases. It would sure make life simple. A fellow wouldn't have to worry about anything. Whatever happened was going to happen.

Wait, I must be nuts, he thought. The things I did tonight, for instance. I had to make myself do them. *But what if they are already written in these books?* He shivered at the idea, it was so spooky. Is it written that he climbed the vine? If so, then the whole universe is mad. His mind was dizzy. He pulled himself together. There could be only one answer—*The History of Tomorrow* was a fake. It *had* to be. It—

Clang! Clang! Matt almost jumped out of his boots. The big door at the end of the room vibrated. The iron bolts were being slid aside. Someone was entering. Trapped! What to do? Matt just hoped that he could think up a good excuse for being where he was.

The door slowly opened. A figure moved out of the shadows and into the room. Great Jumping Jupiter! It was the last person Matt expected to see, or wanted to see. It was the traitor himself: Hector Hornblower!

Matt's first impulse was to punch him right in the nose. But that would come later. Right now it was not a part of his plan. When the Moonster spoke to him in the Bolunkan tongue, Matt knew that his disguise was working.

"Hey," Hector said, "you must be on guard duty here. The Great Klunkus wants a book. The one with the spotted green cover."

Matt tried to fade back into a dark corner. "Yes, sir. You'll find it on one of the desks, I guess."

Hector rummaged around among the papers. "Here it is." He picked up a notebook. "Spotted green cover, all right. Can't read the language, though. Just to make sure, what is this title?"

Anxious to get rid of Hector before he recognized him and sounded an alarm, Matt obliged. He was wearing the glasses. He looked at the book and read aloud, *"Chapter Forty-four. How the Bolunkan Pirates Invade the Moon." Invade the Moon?* He almost choked on the words.

At first Hector didn't notice Matt's reaction. He patted the notebook. "Yeah, that's the baby. But there's gonna be a subtitle: *With the Help of Hector Hornblower, Prince of the Galaxy, Heir to the Throne of Bolunkus, and Consort of the Princess Annalunkus, Long May She Wave."*

The innocent look on Matt's face faded; he just couldn't keep it up. He looked daggers at his countryman. Hector noticed, and remarked, "Say, fella, you seem a little unhappy. The Great Klunkus don't like that, you know."

Matt forced a smile.

"Prince Hector don't like it, neither," the double-crossing Moonster continued. He came closer. "Say, you're awful short and pasty for a Bolunkan."

Matt threw down his hat, and took off the glasses.

Hector backed up, his eyes wide with fright. "Hey, you ain't no punstable, you're—you're—*Looney!*"

"Hornblower, you purple-bellied scoundrel! You—"

Hector dashed for the door, but Matt beat him to it, slamming it shut.

"Looney!"

Hector back-pedaled some more. "Now, wait, I can explain everything."

"That would be an interesting explanation—mutiny, treason, piracy, sending your own fellow Moonsters to prison. And now, an invasion of our Moon. Don't we have enough trouble already with *Earth*?"

"But Matthew—er, Commander Looney, it all depends on your point of view, don't you see? Now, I don't see no treason. I just see it as me helping our starsick people to find their way back to their beloved Moon, when—"

"Knock it off, Hornblower. I have no time to listen to your blubbering baloney. I'm going to lock you up here while I get on with my business." Matt leaped and grabbed him around the neck, but the other fought back, and they ended up rolling around on the floor.

"You—let go!" breathed Hector, struggling.

"Get—in—here!" Matt was trying to force his enemy toward a closet door. They grunted and groaned. Matt was on top, and seemed to be winning.

Then a voice yelled, "Leave him alone!"

Startled, both Moonsters stopped fighting and looked up. The iron door was open. There stood Annalunkus. In her hand was the solar gun. She waved it. "And this time it's loaded," she said. "Now, up against the wall, or I'll fire!"

17. The Princess Takes Sides

Slowly, breathing heavily, the two Moonsters got to their feet and backed against the side of the room.

The Princess peered at Matt. "You look like the Space Commander. Why are you in that uniform?"

"He's dangerous!" Hector cried. "He just escaped from prison. Fear not, my Princess, I shall protect you."

Matt's heart fell. He saw his plans going sky-high. But he couldn't quit now. A bold move was called for. He had nothing to lose, anyway. He took a step toward the girl. "Here, Princess, may I have my gun back, please?"

"Watch out!" Hector warned. "Dear Annalunkus, my future bride, your brave prince will rescue you from evil." But he didn't move.

Matt walked closer, holding out his hand. His eyes met those of Annalunkus. "I shall not hurt you," he promised. She raised the solar gun and aimed it.

"Annalunkus," Hector said, "we shall be so happy, just you and me, in our castle. Your father was so right, in choosing a handsome chap like me as your companion and royal consort. I ain't like other Moonsters, you will find. And just think, I'm all yours."

Matt saw Annalunkus tighten her finger on the trigger. Well, here it comes, he thought, bracing himself, and closing his eyes. A blast of heat and light shot from the muzzle of the solar gun. Matt winced and opened his eyes. Hector Hornblower crumpled to the floor, his ears steaming. Annalunkus let the gun fall to the floor. "I've been wanting to do that for a long time."

"Whew!" Matt sighed. "You had me worried." He looked at the unconscious Moonster. "He'll be all right after a while." He carefully reached down and picked up his solar gun, placing it in the empty holster he had been wearing. She made no attempt to stop him.

"Tell me, why did you do it?"

"You heard what he said. Daddy has us paired. I can't stand the guy. I just hope that you Moonsters will escape from Bolunkus, and that will solve my problem."

"Don't you worry, we'll take him with us when we go," Matt said.

"No, no," Annalunkus protested. "I don't mean that at all."

"What do you mean?"

"Take *me* with you."

"You?" Matt exclaimed. "You're going to run away again?"

"This time for good," the Bolunkan girl said. "I must. You see, on Bolunkus everything has been settled already. That's why I came here, to look in *The History of Tomorrow* to see how much time I have left." She searched the room until she found what she was looking for. "Here it is. Just finished. *Chapter Sixty: Princess Annalunkus Says Yes to Prince Hector.*"

"You don't really believe everything in *The History of Tomorrow,* do you?" Matt asked.

"Of course. There it is, in black and white."

"But you make your future for yourself. No one— no futurian—can do it for you." Matt was arguing for his own peace of mind, too, because he surely wanted Chapter Forty-four to be wrong. He remembered something. He reached deep into a pocket and pulled out the galactic cards; he had carried them through thick and thin. "Here. I'll foretell your future. Ask the cards what you want to know." He shuffled.

"Must I marry him?" She pointed to the body on the floor.

Matt dealt seventeen cards, one by one, placing them

in the wizard circle. Four of fish, nine of crabs, five of murtle, two of groat, and so on. He intoned the magic words:

> "Tell me true, O cards of mine,
> Help me read a future sign:
> For Annalunkus, is there hope?
> Or will she marry this awful dope?"

The Princess looked at the cards, wondering.

"See," Matt said, "on the edge, a five over four. And there, all red. Quick, Annalunkus, when were you born, and how old are you?"

"Um, on the quarter crescent. I'm ten annums, going on twenty."

"Yes, yes," Matt said, poking the cards with his forefinger, "that proves it. Groat against fish, with a zebar rising."

"Proves what?" Annalunkus asked, eyes wide, spellbound by the spooky scene.

"Your happiness is assured. You will make your own choice of a husband. The cards say it, and so be it!" Matt put the magic pasteboards back in his pocket. He hoped she wouldn't ask more questions. He didn't know the answers.

"That isn't what the book says."

"The book says one thing, my cards say another," Matt declared. "Don't you see? Nobody really knows what your future will be, so you have to decide it for

Matt dealt seventeen cards, one by one.

yourself. And running away isn't going to do any good."

Annalunkus stared out the window into the black Bolunkan night for some time. Finally she turned to Matt and smiled. "Well, I hope you are right, Matthew. I'll stay and give it a try." She tossed Chapter Sixty into a trash basket.

"Good!" Matt clapped his hands. "And now I'm going to rescue my friends from their dungeon prison. The sooner we get on our way through space again, the better, and the sooner we'll have Hector out of your hair forever. Will you help?"

Annalunkus smiled. "Of course, I'll help. It's my future, isn't it?"

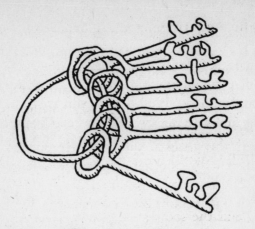

18. The Revolution

With the Princess on his side, things were looking up for Commander Matthew Looney of the Moon Space Navy. First, she helped shut Hector in the closet. He snored loudly. She then volunteered to get the master keys from the guardroom, where she had often seen them hanging on a special hook.

"Be careful," Matt warned. They could hear the sounds of carousing coming from the banquet hall. "I'll wait here."

The girl slipped out. Matt bolted the door. While waiting, he rummaged around the room. When he came across some supplies that included fine parchment, the royal seal, and some wax, he had a brainstorm. He sat at one of the desks, put on the glasses, and took up a writing instrument. He scratched some Bolunkan words back and forth on the parchment. Finished with that, he melted the wax, and pressed the royal seal into it in the lower left corner of the document. After it had dried, he held it up, quite pleased with his handiwork. It looked very official.

There was a rap at the door. He opened it and let Annalunkus in. She happily rattled a large ring with about a dozen huge keys on it.

"Wonderful! How did you manage it?"

"No trouble at all. I simply took them, while the Chief Punstable joked and bowed." She saw the parchment in Matt's hand. "What have you there?"

He handed it to her. She read aloud: "I, Klunkus the Great, hereby resign as Governor of Bolunkus, and appoint Zinkus to rule in my place until a proper election can be held."

Annalunkus looked at Matt sadly. "Oh."

"It has to be done, Princess. Piracy in the cosmos, and prisoners at home—well, it's just not right."

"I know it. I've always known it. I guess that's one reason I run away a lot. But—you won't hurt Daddy, will you?"

"Of course not." Matt rolled up the resignation and tucked it in one pocket, the keys in the other. He put the punstable hat back on. "Come on, we're going to get him to sign it."

As they neared the banquet hall, the sounds of revelry echoed through the passageways of the palace. They came out on a small alcove, where a balcony from on high overlooked the noisy scene. Matt and the girl watched in astonishment. Half the pirates were knocked out cold, lying on the tables, on the floor, or in heaps of two or three, where they had collapsed. The others were jumping up and down, crying strange cries like, "Yaboozin!" and "Riggle-diggle-dumtree!" and "I'm a flippen!" The flippens seemed to be climbing the tapestries, while the yaboozins did somersaults from one end of the long room to the other. A couple of corsairs had somehow climbed onto the big sulphur chandelier that hung from the high ceiling. They had passed out, and their bodies were draped there, while the chandelier swung back and forth slowly.

One by one, the batty buccaneers were falling into a stupor. At the head table, Klunkus was roaring and gulping from a tankard. Captain Morgus lay on the floor, sleeping. Matt took Annalunkus's arm. "Quick, show me the way."

She led him down a narrow spiral stair. They came out behind her father's seat. She put her hand on his shoulder and said, "Daddy." He stopped his singing and turned. Matt saw that his eyes were crossed.

Klunkus looked surprised. "Klunka, my long-lost Klunka, you have come back to me, at last."

147

He wrote KLUNKUS *on the paper.*

"No, Daddy, it's me, Annalunkus, your daughter."

"Are you a flippen?" the befuzzled ruler asked. His head drooped.

Matt had the document unrolled and ready. He quickly spread it on the table under Klunkus's nose. The Princess put a writing stick in her father's hand and said, "Sign here." She held his head.

"Whazzit?" Klunkus asked.

"I'm afraid this means that someone else will sit on the throne, Daddy."

"Oh, that's great, great. The seat's too unfromturbal—comfromturble—umcomfromble—oh, too *hard!*" He wrote KLUNKUS on the paper. His daughter lowered his head gently to the table.

A few moonits later, Matt was behind the wheel of the truck again, the Bolunkan girl with him. Joyously, he sped through the dark roads toward the prison. Oh, that essence of lavaberry! The problems it solved!

"And you, Princess," he told her, "how grateful we Moonsters are."

"I'm not a Princess any more."

"By the way," Matt asked, "who is Klunka?"

"My mother. She used to run away, too. Once she didn't come back. She's out there somewhere. Some day I'm going to find her."

Matt sped up to the prison entrance. With the keys, and with Annalunkus still playing the role of Princess, he had no trouble with the guards. Deep in the cave they found Zinkus waiting with a band of Moonsters and Hotheads ready for action.

It was a triumphal march back to the palace. Matt drove the slosh truck. The new Governor Zinkus stood in the back. He had insisted that Annalunkus be with him, to show that this was a peaceful change from one leader to another. Behind them came the Hotheads, singing "Bolunkus, Gem of the Night," the national anthem which had been banned by Klunkus. Then came a group of Moonsters, ready to do battle for their freedom, if need be.

It was very late at night, yet the marching rebels aroused many Bolunkans from their beds. When they saw and heard what was taking place, many of them joined the throng. Zinkus now knew that he need have no worries about finding supporters. The people were with him. Even the few punstables on duty—those guarding the prison and those walking the streets of the city—quickly joined in. There was laughing and rejoicing, and singing of the battle song, "Sloshing on to Victory."

By the time the great crowd reached the palace, it was daylight. Taking a few Moonsters and Hotheads along, in case there was trouble, Matt, Governor Zinkus, and Annalunkus went inside. The Great Klunkus and his pirates were still unconscious. The

Chief Punstable, when he was shown the official resignation, pledged his loyalty and that of his men to Zinkus. The new Governor stepped onto the front balcony and read the resignation to the people. They cheered. The revolution was over.

A sudden change in government is usually a confusing matter. Zinkus found his hands full with all sorts of official duties and decisions. He used, not the throne, but the main office of the palace, where he sent out many orders and received many visitors.

The Hotheads and their Moonster allies had removed Captain Morgus and the pirates to prison, where they would be kept until they made pledges of allegiance to Zinkus.

Klunkus had been put under house arrest in the palace tower. Later he was to be released, after promising to return to the farm and never enter politics again.

Hector was in solitary confinement in the catacombs under the palace, where he would be held until the moonship was ready to leave.

Annalunkus, who knew quite a lot about government, stayed on as private secretary to Zinkus.

The pirate spaceship was being made into an unarmed passenger and freight vehicle. Whatever booty could be recovered would be returned to its rightful owners in the galaxy, and Bolunkus would pay for the rest.

The Moonsters had moved back onto their space-craft. There was much cleaning up to be done to get ready to continue the voyage to the Hercules Globular Cluster. Harry Stottle, chief engineer of the *Feebey*, probably had the worst job. He had to clean all that canal juice out of the boilers.

"Don't touch a drop of it, or you'll take a trip like you never took before," Matt cautioned him.

Finally, after many, many details had been taken care of, the day came when the moonship was ready to take off, refueled, resupplied, and engines tested. So, Matt made his way to the palace for the last time, to say good-bye. In the executive office at the palace Matt gripped Zinkus's hand. "Farewell, my good friend. If I ever find myself in prison again I'll know whom to call on."

"All I ask is that you think kindly of Bolunkus," Zinkus said, "and come visit us again under more pleasant circumstances."

To Annalunkus, Matt said, "Remember what I told you, young lady, and stay away from those future books."

She squeezed his hand and smiled shyly. "I have one request of you. Daddy wants you to say good-bye to him."

Thus Matt found himself high in the tower where Klunkus was being held. The former ruler had two

reasons for wanting to see Matt. One was to beg for-
giveness for the way he had treated the Moonsters,
which Matt readily gave. The other he quickly re-
vealed.

"Please, Looney, tell me the answer to the riddle. It
has been driving me crazy."

Matt thought about letting the guy suffer, but gave
in. "Ah, yes," he smiled. "What is it that thrives in
winter, dies in summer, and grows upside down? You
haven't guessed it yet?"

"No, no! What's the answer?" Klunkus's feet were
in a pan of water, and it splashed as he became excited.

"Simple enough. An icicle."

Klunkus slapped his knee. "Oh, I should have gotten
it." He laughed. "It's good. If you'd told me, I'd have
let you out of prison."

"I doubt that," Matt replied. "Well, I must go now.
Good luck on the farm."

"By the way," Klunkus said, licking his lips, "you
wouldn't happen to have a little sip of that marvelous
canal juice with you, would you?"

"No." Matt walked out, hoping he'd never see the
Great Klunkus again.

When Matt got back to the spaceport, the last of the
cargo was being loaded. On the bridge of the *Feebey*,
he prepared for takeoff. Mr. Bones checked instruments, especially the mighty astroputer, which would

chart their course. They would soon be ready to go. But one item had not arrived yet. Matt paced the bridge impatiently, until a truck came sloshing across the field. It backed up to the cargo hatch of the *Feebey*. With a winch, crewmen lifted from the truck a box with a small barred window on one side. Printed on the box were the words: *Portable Solitary Confinement Cell.* In it was Hector Hornblower, the traitor. The cell was lowered into the hold of the *Feebey,* and the hatch closed over it.

"I guess that'll hold him, eh, Mr. Bones?" Matt remarked.

"I pray so, Commander."

"All right, Mr. Bones, signal the engine room."

Soon the sound of engine exhausts filled the Bolunkan atmosphere as the *Feebey* lifted off. Matt imagined that he could see his friends on the palace balcony, waving farewell. Despite his experiences there, he left with a feeling of sadness. It was a time he would never forget. The green planet faded into the distance, and Matt finally turned his eyes away and looked ahead.

"Mr. Bones," he ordered, "set your course for the Hercules Globular Cluster."

"Aye, aye, sir."

And this time, Matt told himself, we shall get there.

Epilogue

Commander Looney sat in the mess hall, finishing up a moonburger, his first meal since leaving Bolunkus. It felt good to be back on the familiar *Feebey,* like being closer to home. He munched on the food and made plans for the arrival on Freeholy. The first thing he was going to do was have a jail built and put Hector Hornblower in it. But then a sudden thought occurred to Matt. He had completely forgotten that Hector still owned Freeholy! That meant that he would own the land on which the jail was built, and he would own the jail. If he owned the jail, he would certainly have to be given a key to it. Hector would be free to roam Freeholy and cause all sorts of trouble.

Great Jumping Jupiter! Matt thought. *Am I never*

*going to get this space rat out of my hair? I should
have just left him there on Bolunkus. By the time he
found his way to Freeholy by himself, the time limit
on his deed to the little planet would run out.*

Matt had a few ideas, such as getting his hands on
the deed and tearing it up. That would be silly, because
there was a copy in the files back on the Moon. Or
landing on another planet instead. That would be
taking a chance, because he didn't know anything
about living conditions anyplace but on Freeholy. He
finally decided that the best way was to reason with
Hector. If Hector would cooperate, Matt would speak
up for him when he finally went on trial for treason,
and try to get him off easier. Matt ate up his moonburger
and got ready to leave.

Wondervon Brown came through the galley door.
"Well, Commander, we sail once more, yah?"

"Right, and I want to thank you for your help."

"Dot's okay, even though you did wrinkle mine
apron, und lose mine ladle."

"I've been reading your cookbook. It's good."

"Ock, now you want I autograph, yah?"

"Certainly. I'll bring it with me next meal. Right
now I have an important duty—to move Hornblower
to the brig and try to talk him into being a nice guy."

"Ock, you watch out for dot rotten nebble."

"Don't worry."

*"I have an important duty—to move
Hornblower to the brig."*

A few moonits later Matt was climbing down the steep ladder into the ship's hold. Two crewmen were with him, carrying a gun and rope, just in case Hector acted up. The cargo space was jammed with boxes, bags, bottles, and all sorts of supplies. Matt squeezed through till he came upon the portable solitary confinement cell. He squinted through the small window, but it was dark inside and he couldn't see Hector. He heard him moving about, though.

"Well, Prince Hector, we'll have you out of here in a jiffy," Matt said. He motioned to a crewman. "Okay, open it up."

One sailor took a hammer and began pulling the nails out of one side of the cell. The other Moonster kept his gun ready. Finally, with a crash, the side fell off, and Matt could see inside. There was the prisoner, bent over and cramped. Matt's eyes popped. The sailors dropped gun and hammer with a clatter.

"Well, I'll be a murtle's uncle!" one of them cried.

"You!" Matt exclaimed.

Out of the box stepped—not Hector—but a girl with long red hair, dark skin, a big smile, and bare feet. It was Annalunkus, former Princess of Bolunkus.

"Hi," she said, stretching.

"B-b-but, how?" the surprised Space Commander stammered. "Where's Hector?"

"Back home. Governor Zinkus threw him in prison,

and he'll be there for a good long while. So I changed places with him. Didn't tell you because I thought you wouldn't like it. You're not mad, are you?"

"Well, I guess not," Matt said weakly. "But it sort of mixes me up a little."

"Why?" she asked.

"Oh, you wouldn't understand. It's about a deed that Hector has, and this planet we're going to, and— it's too complicated to explain."

"You mean this?" Annalunkus pulled a document from the carribag she had with her.

Matt recognized it. "That's it! How did you get it?"

"It's mine. Hector gave it to me. I talked to him about it. He's really a nice guy."

"Yeah. Sometimes he's a nice guy but sometimes he isn't," Matt grumbled.

"And he signed it over to me," Annalunkus went on.

"Signed it over to you?"

"That's right. Look." She unfolded the paper, and Matt read where she pointed.

I, Hector Hornblower, herewith relinquish all my rights to the aforementioned planet Freeholy and assign them to Annalunkus Klunkus.

"What the—?" Matt was dumbfounded. "Do you know what this means?"

"Of course," the girl smiled. "I now own Freeholy. And I can't wait to get there. Let's go!"

THE END